THE JOBBER

A *LANCE GEDRIN* MYSTERY

GREG
GOUNTANIS

RB
ROWDY BOOKS

Published by Rowdy Books

Ebook ISBN: 978-1-953762-07-8

Paperback ISBN: 978-1-953762-06-1

Cover design by Deranged Doctor Design

First edition: March 2022

THE LANCE GEDRIN SERIES

1

I was smitten for the umpteenth time. Henri was my witness. When you rescue a Doberman from his old serial killer jefe, he tends to take sides.

We were at the San Antonio Riverwalk on a sweaty August morning. I wanted to escape training camp for my next fight and Henri wanted to make friends with the ducks. He tugged on his leash, got down on all fours, and inched his nose toward the edge of the water. The ducks played hard to get, but knowing Henri, he had a backup plan. If perchance the ducks quacked in his direction, Henri would join them. He was a natural swimmer and a natural boss. He'd lead the pack downstream, and I'd be hyperventilating every step of the way.

Unfortunately, I didn't possess any snorkeling game, and I was several fries short of a happy meal when it came to floating, diving, plunging, and the like. I gripped Henri's leash so tight it should have complained. He kept his gaze on the ducks, so I tried another tack.

"Let's go get some food," I said.

Henri ate it up.

He stood ramrod straight like a soldier at roll call and gazed into my eyes so long I felt bad for making him wait. I rummaged in my pocket and gave him the lone remaining duck biscuit left.

"I'll stock up on the way home, don't worry."

Henri gazed at me less enthusiastically this time and we continued down the riverwalk. We'd been at it for the last fifteen minutes, and I was feeling thirsty.

I was approaching one of the food and drink stands when I saw her.

No more than twenty paces in front of me. Five-foot-five, a shade over one hundred twenty pounds, chiseled frame, with beige Ray-Bans. She wore a gray pair of joggers, a black tee with words I couldn't quite place, and white trainers. Her brunette locks were pulled back in a short ponytail, and she moved with a purpose.

I paid for my water bottle and took Henri in her direction. I didn't want to make it obvious that I was enamored by her trainers so I held back a few paces and examined the foliage on the path. The joggers girl seemed lost in thought. She was examining the water and the pedestrian bridges in the distance. At one point she stopped by a bench, tied her shoes with one hand, stretched out her hamstrings and kept going. Looking, smiling, closing her eyes, and repeating. It went like that for several minutes. In an age when the average woman was tethered to her fruit phone waiting for all the small boxes to pop up and ping, it was refreshing to see a woman appreciate the great outdoors.

Henri got sick of my analysis, so he rolled on his back and curled his paws up in a fetal position. I smiled and rubbed him fully. I reached for a treat, but then remembered I needed to get him some more. My mind did that sometimes. Forgetfulness was a thing in the fight game.

I tugged on Henri's leash and we kept walking in the direction of the joggers girl. She was a solid thirty paces in front, and the path was starting to fill up with more tourists. The sun was getting heavier so I had some water and then trudged on. I had no idea what I would say if I eventually crossed paths with her and made a comment about her trainers. I tended to go with the flow when it came to male-female interactions. Truth be told, my record with the female sex was the greatest parabola of all time. I gained and lost significant others like a bout of influenza. Maybe it had to do with the fact that I broke people's skulls for a living, or that I was a nomad in a new motel in a new state of the union the majority of the time.

If that wasn't it, then maybe it was the fact that I'd done twelve years for a murder I didn't commit and came damned close to getting a three-drug cocktail that would have stopped my heart forever before I was sprung on a technicality.

That's why spontaneity is such a beautiful thing. If the joggers girl wanted to talk, then I'd talk. If not, then so be it. Henri would get some pets and we'd be on our way. Complicating matters was that I was a celebrity of sorts. I tried to lay low because of all the gawkers and media hombres, yet I was ever the optimist with each new interaction. Perhaps things would click in the Lone Star State and I'd meet a mesmerizing nomad who had a thirst for more.

Till then, I'd take my crookeds with the straights.

The joggers girl was ten feet away, turning toward one of the pedestrian bridges. Perhaps the real reason I wanted to chat with her was because I could have sworn I'd met her before. I couldn't quite place it, but I knew deep down that we'd crossed paths at some point, and I needed to assuage my curiosity.

Ten seconds later, everything changed.

The joggers girl walked up the bridge, and when she got about halfway, she was surrounded by a bunch of goons. Three in front, and three from behind. If I had to make a hypothesis, they were a mini bling ring going up and down the riverwalk taking shit off all the tourists. Hard-ass wannabes who needed to be put in their place.

I loosened my grip on Henri's leash and clenched my right fist. I was playing all the scenarios in my head, and they all involved a heavy dose of carnage inflicted by me upon the wannabes. I could take them all out in about eleven seconds flat if I was efficient. If I was less than efficient, it'd take me about thirteen seconds, and if I was having a bad day, it'd take me about twenty seconds, and by then my actions would grab the attention of more passersby, deterring the wannabes from coming back for more.

My plan was to keep it relatively civilized. I'd throw a few over the water, break a couple noses and ribs, and I'd let the last hombre run back home to Mama. The fight game was muy bueno.

I smiled as the violent thoughts swirled in my head.

But none of it mattered.

The joggers girl did all the work for me. One of the wannabes stepped toward her and she roundhouse kicked him to the face. The dude was seeing a plethora of sheep. Then she slipped a wobbly punch and left hooked another dude into next week. One wannabe ran off, and the three on the other side of the bridge all charged at her in a triangular formation. Strength in numbers. Hell no. The joggers girl caught one dude in a chokehold and put him to sleep in seconds. Then she delivered a crisp uppercut to one of the other dudes. The third got such a hard liver shot I could see his stomach shaking for an eternity. There was no way he'd ever be able to consume another sip of alcohol.

She was more than efficient. It took her ten seconds to dispatch all the wannabes. I kept count in my head. When it was all done, she dusted off her black tee and picked her phone up off the ground. She dusted that off too and put it back in her pocket. I could see some tourists farther down the walkway clapping, but the joggers girl ignored them.

I'd seen enough, and apparently so had Henri. He pulled me onto the bridge and ran up to the woman, wagging his tail back and forth.

The joggers girl snapped out of it and smiled.

"So cute," she said, rubbing Henri's whiskers.

I was smitten.

"He's drawn to badass women," I said.

She laughed, and I knew right then and there I'd definitely met her before.

"Lance Gedrin," I said, putting my hand out.

She raised her eyebrows. "We still do that nowadays?" She lifted her elbow and made like she was gonna give me an elbow dab.

I pulled my hand back and moved for an elbow dab too, but she stopped me at the last second.

"Just fucking with you, Gedrin," she said.

She shook my hand.

"How could I miss the heavyweight champ of the world checking me out and using his dog as a chick magnet?"

I usually had a witty reply to everything, but sometimes you gotta fall on your sword.

"Preach, mystery woman," I said.

She smiled.

"Hayley Devin, but you know that already."

It all clicked.

I knew we'd met before.

Hayley Devin was the former UFC flyweight champion of the world. I'd seen her achieve some of the most brutal knock-outs in the octagon. She dribbled people's heads off the cage, and many of her foes were too fucked up to ever fight again. I'd never met her in person, but there's an intimacy on the television screen that never goes away.

"Imagine that," I said. "Two champs on the same bridge at the same time in the Lone Star State."

"Does that work with all the girls?"

"Just the champs," I said.

Devin gave me a playful push, then she petted Henri again.

"What brings you out here?"

"I'm dodging camp and making my way to the Sand Dunes to sled. They have some really high peaks in Colorado." I told her about the bucket list that I'd established since I'd gotten out of the joint and how I wanted to hit up new spots as much as I could.

"The Dunes suck, but dodging camp, I dig that."

I never changed an item on my list for anybody, so I knew right then and there that it'd be just me and Henri on the slopes.

"And what brings you out here, ass kicker?" I said.

Devin rolled her eyes. "Was in Austin taking in the sights, but then I have this damned presser for my next fight tonight in this rickety gym down here in San Antonio, so I came a little early. I'm with a smaller promotion since the big boys dropped me."

"The struggle is real," I said. "Good left hook by the way."

"I learned from the best."

We shared a laugh, but it didn't last long.

Devin got a text on her phone and everything changed.

2

Devin collapsed in my arms and started hyperventilating. I did a great job breaking her fall, and I did what any hombre would do in that situation: I stood still like a statue and waited for things to correct themselves. I didn't excel at therapeutics and had learned long ago that canines were better suited for that purpose.

Twenty seconds later things calmed down. Devin broke free, and she showed me her phone.

The text read, *STOP SINGING, JAKEY BOY*.

All caps.

And the message got worse. Right below it was a picture of a man in his early thirties, gagged and tied to a chair. He had a bruise below his right cheekbone, a crooked nose, and he looked like he'd seen a million ghosts. The man's jeans were stained and he was wearing an old-school pro wrestling t-shirt with the word "What?" emblazoned across the front in big white letters —an homage to Stone Cold Steve Austin, perhaps the biggest game-changer in all of pro wrestling.

The edges of the photo were blurry and I couldn't see any

other figures in the background. But I felt for the gagged man. He was a rookie caught up in trouble, and he looked like he had no ounce of fight left in him. He was hanging on for dear life and he needed an out.

I looked at the photo one more time and examined it for any other important details. My brain might have had a penchant for forgetting of late, but in times of duress my odds of remembering seemed to increase. I closed my eyes and took it all in. The gagged man was a member of the tribe, and when a fellow member of the tribe is in trouble, you have to make things right. I had been a huge pro wrestling fan growing up and to this day still drew inspiration from the promos and the storylines. Had there been a pro wrestling school close by me when I was young, I could have easily tossed the boxing gloves for the wrestling trunks.

But things happen for a reason.

Somebody was messing with a member of the club, and I'd get to the bottom of it. My mind ran rampant with ideas on how to save the hombre.

Then Devin upped the ante.

"That's my autistic brother," she said.

We found a bench and sat down.

"Jake's forty," she continued. "Looks all big and macho on the outside, but he's really a teddy bear. The Asperger's makes him fixate on things all the time. Stats and colors and all that wrestling shit. I keep telling him it's all fake, but he lives in a different city upstairs and that's that. No changing him now."

"There's a fine line between genius and insanity," I said. "Sincerely, a famous writer."

Devin rolled her eyes.

I tried another tack.

"Who was watching him?" I said.

"Momma was his caretaker till she passed from COPD. He

got another one after that, and she's been with him ever since. Same house for the last forty years. Same room. But leave it to sis to come take him away for the weekend and get him fucking kidnapped. I left him back at the hotel to come walk this morning."

Devin buried her head in her hands, and I rubbed her shoulders. It took her a few seconds to get present again, then she wiped away some smears of makeup on her cheek and stood back up.

She started walking down the bridge, and I followed with Henri.

"You have any beefs?" I said.

My amateur sleuth radar never fizzled. It didn't take a rocket scientist to get to the bottom of it all. First start with the usual suspects: crazy exes, bookies, irked family members. Follow up on all leads, cross them out as you see fit, and piece the puzzle together. I loved the gig.

Devin stared at the water and balled her fists. "Only one asshole who would do something like this. Anton Tens. My asshole former agent. Shady and manipulative and always doing things behind my back."

"What a shyster."

Devin nodded. "After I lost my belt, the UFC wasn't giving me good fights anymore. Anton would try and get me on some prelims and shit, but I knew I still had main event in me. I knew I had a lot left in the tank. So I fired his ass and found a different promotion. All on my own. No suits or nothing."

Devin gesticulated as she talked, and the more she did so, the more I was drawn in. She had grace and beauty and power and apparently an entrepreneurial spirit too. I wanted to enjoy this ride for as long as it lasted, and I wanted to get her brother back. Plain and simple.

"Bellator?" I said.

"No. An upstart called FCL. Fight Champions League. I negotiated a three-fight deal, all main events. Media exposure isn't as big as the big boys, but they have a good social media team and it's all about streams and shit nowadays. My signing had a million views across all platforms, which is a start. I win this first fight and I get a hella bonus."

I smiled. My agent, Mark Sims, loved to talk about the business aspect of the fight game, and I routinely tuned him out. I just wanted to break skulls and get paid. But Devin had a way of making you excited even if it wasn't your bonus that was on the line. I genuinely wanted her to get rewarded for the fruits of her labor because the bottom line was that every fighter that stepped in the ring risked never coming out of it. It was life and death every minute. So good for her to get paid and to do it without the shysters getting a big-ass cut of the pie.

"Anton is a shrewd bitch," Devin said. "Even though he didn't negotiate my deal, he knows all the standard clauses. I have the presser tonight and if I miss it, I don't get paid and the fight next month is off. Breach of contract. Standard legalese. I couldn't get the damned suits to cut that part out. So Anton has a reason to set up all this shit with my brother."

I finished my water and tossed it along the way. Legalese was my middle name, but I let the thought pass into the ether as we kept walking. The heat was really picking up and I felt my t-shirt sticking more and more. The crowd seemed to multiply on the riverwalk and the sun was shining harder on the cobblestone. Henri was thirsty now so I stopped along the walk, bought another water bottle and asked for a bowl. One of the proprietors gave me a Styrofoam bowl and Henri didn't mind at all.

"He's really well behaved," Devin said.

"He's the quintessential service dog," I said.

"Let me guess. His master has head maladies?"

She was good.

"Among other things."

Devin smiled and we kept on.

Life is filled with a plethora of ups and downs. Certainty and uncertainty jockey for position as the days turn into nights and the cycle repeats itself. I wasn't a perfect man by any means, but I was introspective. I knew all my tics and quirks, and I was proud of it. I was a very self-aware person.

And once I latched on to something, I had to see it through. Like a junkie on speed, there was no tomorrow. I had no idea where Jake was, but dammit, I was going to find out. I would leave no stone unturned, come hell or high water. I'd known Devin all of a few minutes, but I would do her that solid. She deserved as much.

I'd ask a question and I'd get an answer. Then I'd ask another question and get another answer. The song and dance would go on until some sort of progress was made or all parties got sick and tired of the song and dance.

I'd do it for Devin, but I'd do it for myself too. I embraced the challenge, and I loved winning. I was undefeated as an amateur sleuth, and I intended to keep my crown.

"We need to go straight to the source," I said.

"The source is gone," Devin said. "The message has been sent. Anton may be dumb, but he hides shit really well. My bro's out of the state by now. At least that's what I'd do if I was the kidnapper type."

"Where are you staying?" I asked.

Devin told me, and we left the riverwalk.

If Jakey boy fixated on things, then maybe he was fixated enough to leave a clue behind for his saviors.

Clues made the mystery game go round.

3

Devin's new promotion might have been small, but she had negotiated a suite into her contract. Henri and I didn't have to go far to find it because it sat on the fifteenth floor of one of the hotels smack dab on the riverwalk. Plush beige carpet lined the whole space, the furniture was straight out of the finest catalogs, and the kitchen even had a waffle maker. I was still team pancake through and through, but I respected the breakfast tools on display.

Devin pushed past me and started searching all the rooms. If she had the blues when she got the mysterious text earlier, she had completely eviscerated them on the walk over. She had a steely resolve now and the look on her face was pure business. I walked toward the bedroom first, but that didn't do the space justice.

The suite was a two-bedroom layout, with a king bed in one room and two double beds in the other. We went into the room with the double beds first.

"Jake needs to sleep next to people," Devin said. "He sees

things at night, so the caretaker always had an inflatable bed right next to him. When we came out here I wanted to duplicate the experience."

"Best to soothe," I said.

Devin nodded. I joined the search of the double bedroom. I went to the windowsill first and looked for any signs of forced entry. Apart from some grime in the upper corners of the window, it was pristine and untouched. Nobody had used the window anytime recently.

I looked out over the riverwalk for anything out of the ordinary. When nothing caught my eye, I turned back to the room. Devin was flipping her brother's mattress.

"He's too big to hide under there," I said.

"No shit, Sherlock. Maybe he left his phone."

"Touché."

I helped Devin with the other side of the mattress. We hoisted it up and tossed it to the side. We did the same with the box spring. But we came up empty. The bedding was well-kept. We put everything back together and repeated the process with the other bed.

Nada.

I started riffling through the dresser. It had a large mirror attached to it and eight pull-out drawers, four on each side. An extended traveler's dream. I went through them carefully. Jake had some wrestling t-shirts in a couple of the drawers and some phone chargers, but that's all she wrote. The yellow pages filled the top left-hand drawer, and some food menus sat in the top right.

"He keeps everything in his suitcase," Devin said. "But it was getting stinky so I made him take some stuff out."

"The kid is a very good listener."

"He better be. If he wants to make it out of this alive."

She said it matter-of-fact, but I knew the subtext. The unspoken word. If Jake tried to get cute with his kidnappers or he didn't follow the rules to the letter, he was fucked. He'd never watch another episode of *Smackdown* again.

Devin was keeping it all together. That was part of the fighter's DNA, after all. When the world is nothing but noise on the outside, stay centered and don't show any sign of weakness. My trainer Sal would chew my ass out if my eyes opened wider than they should in the ring. Weakness is best friends with your fucking eyes. Keep them narrow and focused, boyo.

Yep.

"Toss his bag," I said.

Devin picked up Jake's suitcase, which sat in the corner of the room. It was the carry-on wheel type. She unzipped it and went through each compartment. When she came up empty she lifted it up and shook it. No phone came out.

I went to the living room next. I didn't expect the kid to pop outta the cushions, but I expected to find something of import. That's how the game worked. A famous Hollywood type once said, "The harder I work, the luckier I get."

Preach. The more I worked, the more I'd get. Plain and simple.

I started tossing the couch cushions. I reached my hand in all the crevices, and when that yielded nothing, I hoisted the couch up on two of its legs. The cleaning ladies had neglected some Jolly Rancher wrappers, but that was it. More nada. For good measure, I hoisted the couch up from the other side as well, but that was just as unproductive.

I repeated the process for all the furniture in the living space. Look, fish, lift. I came up short each time and went to the kitchen. I was hungry and was tempted to wolf down a banana that sat in a fruit bowl on the counter. I stared it down for several seconds. My potassium levels were low at times.

Another one of Sal's humdinger diagnoses. But I had a job to do.

I pocketed the banana for the road and searched the whole kitchen space. Cabinets, drawers, the fridge itself, and the freezer. Hell, I even checked the two small cabinets atop the fridge. Nothing important. Then I turned to the final piece in the space. The waffle maker. I respected the fact that Devin had one, but I still knew I would never make the shift full-time to that breakfast delicacy. I was a pancake connoisseur and some things just never change.

I opened up the waffle maker out of curiosity and was relieved to find that Devin perhaps shared the same taste as me. The maker was pristine and unused, the instruction booklet still inside.

I smiled, closed the maker, and walked back to Devin. She was in the master bedroom riffling through things.

"Let's get out of here," she said. "This was a colossal waste of time." She was biting her nails.

"No treasures?" I said.

She rolled her eyes.

"If at first you don't succeed, bring in the hounds."

She didn't get the reference. I walked back into Jake's room, took one of his t-shirts, and came back.

"Henri, come."

Henri had been lying down on the kitchen tile from the moment we'd walked in, spent from the walk and the heat. But he really was the best, no matter the circumstances. When he heard his name, he sprinted to the bedroom and stood still. I let him smell Jake's shirt for a few seconds.

"Henri, go find it."

Henri wagged his tail and started searching throughout the place.

"Won't he hit on anything that Jake touched?" Devin said.

"Yes, but he'll hit on things we can't see."

"Damn, you're smarter than I gave you credit for, champ."

"I'm all about that side hustle."

Henri hit on Jake's suitcase, shirts, socks, shoes, and even the waffle maker. Each time he hit on something he'd pause, sit right next to it, and bark. I'd give him praise and then Henri would carry on like a boss. He went at it for several minutes.

"We should call the coppers," Devin said. "I appreciate the assist here, but they can track Anton's ass the right way."

I looked at Henri and knew he was determined to find something important. He kept searching.

"The only things the coppers can track are the number of bullshit tickets they need each month to meet their quota."

I pulled up the king mattress and didn't see anything. I motioned to Devin and we did what we did in the other bedroom. We hoisted, flipped, and searched. Nothing doing. Then I got down on my stomach and looked underneath. I was batting zero for the whole day.

Devin examined the dresser in the room, and I examined the nightstand. And that's when I got lucky. Henri sprinted over next to me, sat down, and barked.

"What is it?" I said.

Henri barked again.

"He's getting tired," Devin said.

"He's on his game. Wait."

I unplugged the yellow table lamp that sat atop the stand and put it aside. Then I picked up the nightstand and shook it. The quality of the wood was subpar, and small wood chunks fell out the bottom.

I looked at Henri. He barked again.

Many service dogs lost their abilities over time. Like an aging athlete who thinks he still has it, the fall is usually a series of hits and misses, but more misses. Then it becomes swift and saddening and the critics say the athlete is a shell of his former self and should call it quits for good.

Henri wasn't there yet.

Because when I ran my hand under the nightstand, a cell phone was taped up against the base.

4

I gave Henri my banana for his efforts, and he gobbled it up faster than you could say banana. I pulled the phone off the nightstand and did away with the tape. Devin smiled at me, and I returned it.

Jake's phone was old-school. A silver Motorola Razr with a Vans sticker on the front. I knew the phone was a first generation because I had tried swinging a deal for the same one when I got out of Pontiac. A suave salesman in Chicago had done his best to sell me a top-of-the-line fruit phone, but I'd wanted something foldable. I told him about all the commercials circa 2004 and how the silver Razr really glistened in one's palm. The crème de la crème of mobile technology. The hombre looked at me like I had the plague and then broke the news that the Razr didn't come with buttons anymore. It was touch-screen or bust these days. Long story short, I stood firm in my quest for buttons, and thus the Jitterbug with all its portly glory won out. It's been my non-fruit phone of choice ever since.

In short, I was liking Jake more and more. The kid had a

classic way about him, and when I found him I'd tell him as much.

Devin took the Razr out of my hands and peeled off the sticker.

"He's obsessed with multi-colored things," she said. "The sticker covers the damned flap."

I hadn't paid much attention to the sticker, but when I looked at it again the sticker did in fact cover the flap. Every time Jake wanted to use the phone the sticker would have to be peeled off the flap and then reattach itself.

"The mind is a trip," I said.

Devin shook her head and started pressing buttons on the phone. She was dedicated to the cause and pressed away for a good minute straight. But the screen didn't light up. I took a stab at it and tried pressing the buttons in combos she didn't press, but it was more of the same. Jake's phone was shot.

I walked around the room looking for a charger. There wasn't one in the master bedroom so I went back to the double bedroom and opened the eight-drawer nightstand from earlier. The chargers in there didn't match a phone though.

"Those are for his tablet," Devin said.

I shook my head and looked around the room again. I picked up the mattress and the box spring on both beds once again, undid the sheets and the pillowcases, but came up empty.

Devin was biting her nails again, and right on cue Henri went over to her side. If his finder skills from earlier didn't showcase his talents enough, his soothing qualities did. A service dog has no limits. In times of strife or unease he or she can pick up on all the cues that humans can't. And can make every human melt in a matter of seconds.

Henri nestled his head into Devin's left thigh, and she had no choice but to pull the rascal close and give him some love.

She rubbed his whiskers and scratched his belly. Then she picked him up and gave him a big hug. Henri loved every second of it. He licked her face and tackled her on the bed.

I smiled and went back to the master bedroom. The king bed had a solid merlot wood frame, and the sheets were far silkier than the ones across the hall. I ran my hands under the comforter in case a charger was hiding somewhere. I came up empty, and I ran my hands under the covers too. Same thing.

I was about to walk back into the living area when I found it.

Right beside the TV, hanging out of one of the new USB ports, but tucked in back of the monitor. A charger. People were too cool for outlets these days. I pulled it out of the TV and walked back across the hall. Henri's therapeutics were over and he was sprawled out on Jake's bed, napping. Devin was examining a clunky piece of hotel art on the wall.

I showed her the charger and she held up her hands.

"That's a dead end, champ," she said.

She pointed to the very large extension on the end of the charger and the very small hole going into the bottom of the Razr. She was right on the money.

"How many tablets does this kid have?" I said.

Devin laughed, then punched me in the shoulder.

"Just playing. Here." She pulled another cord out of her pocket and tossed it to me. It was some sort of adapter. I looked it over for a few seconds trying to figure it out before finally getting it.

I set it up, then I plugged in the phone and the screen lit up like a million Christmas trees. A passcode was needed though.

"He knows not to lock his stuff," Devin said. Her face got red for the first time and she balled up her fists. For a moment I thought she was gonna throw a jab out of reflex.

I liked her even more.

"No biggie," I said. "Start with the usual suspects."

I asked Devin for birthdates, hobbies, sports teams, school mascots, and more to get the codes. She provided everything with ease. She really knew Jake well, but the phone kept shaking and spitting out error messages.

We stood there in silence for a few seconds, then it dawned on me that if Jake was all about the wrestling business, he wouldn't shy away from that when it came to protecting his phone. The casuals were intimidated out of admitting they liked pro wrestling. Maybe it was the fact that the storylines were pre-scripted, or maybe they were in fear of being outed for idolizing men in spandex. But those that really bled the business, bled it all over. T-shirts. Posters. Action figures. Video games. The true hardcore fans didn't give a shit about societal norms and expectations.

Jake's password was wrestling-based. I was sure of it. I just had to figure it out.

I racked my brain for what Jake's brain was probably thinking when he set the code. Famous grapplers came to mind and famous storylines and famous periods of pro wrestling lore. But I kept it super simple. Jake liked Stone Cold. I started there and put in some combinations.

Nada.

The gears started churning in my head, and I realized that Jake grew up watching the business when it was in its heyday. When it wasn't a kids' show and wasn't soft on the themes and the gore and the sex and the action.

The attitude era.

That was the heyday of pro wrestling. I got hooked on it, and so did Jake.

The passcode was only six digits, and words were out of the equation. I racked my brain some more. I knew there was a connection to the era, but I couldn't quite place it.

Numbers.

Attitude.

Austin.

3:16.

Don't Trust Anybody.

Vince.

DX.

The Rock.

Mankind.

The Hardy Boyz.

Started in '97.

Ended in 2001.

Then the show became shitty.

Bingo.

The start and end dates for the greatest era in pro wrestling. I put in 9701 to delineate the approximate start date and end date. But I was two digits short. I tried another combo and came up empty.

"He took me to that shit once," Devin said. "So fake sitting up close. It's like they're hitting each other open hand. I get the entertainment part of it, but they couldn't do this shit for real in the octagon."

"Brock did."

I was back to my zingers, and Devin didn't have anything to say about that one. I closed my eyes and thought of more numbers. Wrestling-related. It went like that for a while.

Then I got it.

The t-shirt. Not Jake's t-shirt from the photo. The "What?" shirt was a vintage Austin wrestling t-shirt for sure, but there was another t-shirt perhaps even more vintage and more emblematic of the attitude era.

The Austin 3:16 shirt.

I added it all up, but I had one too many digits.

I took out the 1 in 2001 and put in the code 316970.

The screen hesitated for a second. Then it unlocked.

Jake, you little rascal.

The phone itself was basic. Not many apps, save for some pinball games. I went to the texts section and there were some spammer texts and some old ones from Devin. The missed calls section was more robust. Calls from Devin again, but I also found a bunch of out-of-state numbers. Given the soliciting over the phone these days, that wasn't a surprise. But then I found one repeat number, with five missed calls. All from about an hour ago.

Sleuthing was the best game in town.

I called the number. A low, gravelly voice picked up.

"Brainy boy, where you at?" the voice said.

5

I did my best brainy boy impression. I'd say it was a cross between Urkel and Malcolm in the Middle.

"Waiting for you," I said.

The gravelly voice on the other end of the line snorted.

"Always fucking late. How do we ever do business with you? Get your ass to Lot B," the voice said.

The line went dead.

"I'm gonna kill him," Devin said. "Where's this coming from?"

She sat down at the edge of the bed and rubbed her scalp like she had a migraine.

I rubbed her shoulder again.

"Call the caregiver," I said. "She might have more intel."

Devin got up from the bed, pulled out her phone, and made the call on speaker. The phone rang a bunch of times before going to voicemail.

"This is Maria, I go vacation through Monday. Leave message I call back later."

Devin snapped the phone shut.

"Figures. Can never reach her when it matters."

"Everybody deserves some R and R," I said.

She started pacing all over the room. I wanted Henri to soothe her again, but he was still napping. She stopped in front of me and held her palm out, and I gave her Jake's phone back.

"I appreciate all this, I really do," she said. "But this is getting really weird right now and I can't process it all. It's really freaking me out. I'm calling the cops."

She pocketed Jake's phone and started dialing on hers.

I stopped her.

She stood there, frozen, staring at the phone but not pressing any more buttons.

I looked her up and down, and despite her badass ways, her eyes told of somebody who had been through the wringer. Maybe it was with her mom, or maybe it was her deadbeat dad. Hell, maybe it was the physical and emotional toll of taking care of Jake his whole life. Whatever it was, it was radiating out of her in that moment. I instantly got her and instantly felt for her on a deeper level.

I usually never hesitated to give my opinion on all things under the sun, but now I remained silent.

And waited.

I don't recall how long exactly, but then Devin looked me up and down. Slowly. Deliberately.

"I don't want this to go south," she said. "I wouldn't be able to take it. I'm not as tough as everybody makes me out to be."

"I know," I said.

I gave her a big hug and she took it. We stood there for a very long time.

"When I put something in my mind, it's game on. And I don't lose," I said. I pulled back from her and held her gaze. Two champs with finely honed stare-downs going at it.

Then she put her game face on.

"Let's get the hell out of here," she said. "This place is too extra for me right now."

I snapped my fingers, and Henri woke from his nap and got into a perfect heeling position.

"Where did you get him?" Devin said.

"A magician never reveals his secrets," I said.

"Whatever. And that goes both ways."

She gave me a sly smile, and I started to get excited again. A recipe for disaster. I thought of pancakes and the feeling subsided.

"Probably a hundred Lot B's out here," I said.

Devin shook her head. "Nope. Only one place around here is big enough to name their lots by letters. The convention center."

I went with it. Sometimes a fighting lady knows the ways better than any nomad and his canine could.

We left the suite and found the elevators. Devin's place was literally two steps from the buttons, and I appreciated that. We took the elevator down to the main level. When we left the hotel, I stood by the curb and waited. Henri too.

"Tired already?" Devin said.

"'Tis the loading station for the Ubers," I said. "I saw them pull up here when we came in."

Devin laughed.

"The center is walking distance, champ. Not gonna hurt you to get some steps in before camp."

"Excellent," I said.

Devin shook her head and we all started walking east. Less than ten minutes later we reached the convention center. The space easily spanned half a million square feet, with so many lots and letters that I had a headache just looking at the damn things.

We found Lot B and sat on the outskirts on a bench overlooking all the cars. By the looks of it there weren't any big functions going on. I counted less than thirty cars.

I turned to Devin, who was examining the entryway to Lot B.

"What's the play, champ?" I said.

She threw her hands up, as lost as I was. I'd been an amateur sleuth long enough to realize that when things seem bleak, serendipity is a beautiful thing. It makes the world go round. Professional detectives rely on training and psychology and all those fancy things. Sometimes they get the job done and sometimes they fail miserably.

But I relied on instinct and chance and body language. I knew the score, and I could read people a mile away. Devin and I didn't have to wait long to find out what to do next.

A big white van pulled up to the center of the lot, and a few burly dudes came out. They walked toward some shrubbery and pulled out a pack of smokes. They shared the box and took drags on their cigarettes. They were fucking up their lungs, but they were also buying time talking to each other and pretending to blend in.

For brainy boy.

"That's them," Devin said. She pointed to the portlier dude on the right. I hadn't gotten a good look at the hombres on the bridge earlier, but Devin had undoubtedly gotten up close and personal when she kicked all their candy asses.

She clenched her fists and started moving toward the lot. I held her back.

"No way," I said.

"Get the hell off of me. They have Jake."

"You go within ten feet of that van or those assholes, and Jake's finito. I'll go. They don't know me from the bridge and they don't know this rascal here."

I looked down at Henri, and he turned his head sideways.

She took a step back toward the bench and closed her eyes. She looked like she was visualizing her prey. I did it every time in the ring. See it, feel it, destroy it. Sal trained me the right way, and I'm sure Devin had her fair share of solid trainers over the years too. Octagon or squared circle, dedication is dedication and mental warfare is mental warfare.

"Don't do anything stupid," she said. "Low-key."

I nodded, and walked toward the lot with Henri by my side. Two of the burly hombres had bounced back into the van, but another remained, smoking some Marlboros and talking on his phone. I couldn't quite place the accent, but it surely wasn't an English twang of any sort. It leaned European. Serbian maybe.

He raised his voice on the phone, made eye contact with me, and quickly went back to his conversation. He walked toward some shrubbery and tossed his cigarette butt. Henri took it as his cue to search and find. He pulled on his leash and went toward the spot where the man was.

I expected him to hop up on the concrete ledge, sniff the shrubs where the butt had landed, and bark when he found it. But Henri had tricks up his sleeve. He used the opportunity to piss all over the concrete, just inches from the man's foot.

The man jumped back.

"Fuck," he shouted. "Take care of that thing."

"Easy," I said. "His prior owner was one crazy cookie."

The man gave me a quizzical look.

Then somebody shouted from the van in a language that definitely sounded Serbian.

The man shook his head and ran toward the van. The van screeched away like it was trying to win a medal. Maybe they'd recognized my voice or had spotted Devin up top by the bench.

I didn't care.

I memorized the plate.

6

Devin booked an Uber this time. Henri took his customary position right behind the driver, I took the middle, and Devin took the other side. One of the benefits of being a celebrity—even a C-list one—is that you have a guy for everything. A hair guy. A clothes guy. A tickets guy. A pancakes guy. The list went on ad infinitum. Sims had forged most of this Rolodex of contacts himself over the years, but I'd cultivated my own cool humanoids list too.

Case in point, my vehicle registration Texas dude. I'd called him up and given him the plate of the van, and he'd given me an address. Devin and I were on our way there. The place was just a few miles away.

Problem was, the Uber driver was driving slow as molasses and asking about all my fights under the sun. I normally didn't have an issue boasting about legally beating people's brains in, but truth be told the more time went by the more I forgot shit. My brain cells really were like flimsy french fries sometimes. As much as I didn't like admitting it, we fighters all had an expiration date. Whether bare-knuckle or boxing or MMA or Muay

Thai or whatever, brain damage is brain damage. The accumulation of such damage hits its mark eventually. And there's no reversing it.

I knew of old foes, sparring partners, and old fight-game legends that had croaked due to a variety of maladies: stroke, heart attack, lung cancer, suicide. Father Time was undefeated. I knew my date would come sooner rather than later, but till then I liked to pretend it leaned more toward the latter. So when Uber drivers questioned my fights, I tuned out the majority of it and nodded my head at all the right times and smiled at all the others.

Devin picked up on it.

"Need some Z's there, champ?" she said.

I feigned a snore, and she punched me in the shoulder. Henri turned his head my way for support, then went back to the window.

"The fight game is muy bueno," I told the driver.

He fixed his mirror and looked at me. "How long you practice those kidney shots on Juko?"

I remembered the name, but I hardly remembered the fight. Another spectacle in front of another crowd. Another beat-down probably.

"It's all Greek to me," I said.

The driver laughed, and then fixed his mirror toward Devin. "You should never have been on the ultimate fighter. They should have just given you a fight at straw weight to build from there. The big companies are so corrupt. I'm glad you got out."

"Sex sells," Devin said. "I got the script each week and just wanted to be like J-Law, but my theater chops were reined in by all the suits."

The driver laughed.

The more Devin talked the more enamored I was with her.

She had a tough exterior and a steely interior. She was reeling from Jake, but she didn't show it to the masses. She was witty and gritty and unflappable. An excellent combo.

I shifted a little closer toward her side of the seat, and she moved closer to me till our knees touched. She smiled, and I returned it. Maybe my misfortunes in the love department were about to change. Commonalities are the real deal.

"What's a typical meal like for you?" the driver asked.

"Pancakes and OJ," I said. "With pure maple syrup. None of that high-fructose shit."

"No, silly," Devin said. "Oatmeal and eggs and some branch-chain aminos for recovery and growth."

"You put people in cages and that's what happens," I said. "All this science, like it'll save you from cage burn."

The driver laughed. "My girlfriend wants me to go on a diet, but I refuse to give up my frozen pizzas."

"What kinda toppings?" I asked.

"Sausage and bacon. Sometimes the combo one with green pepper and onion."

"Don't ditch those frozen pizzas, son. Give me carbs or give me death. Hold firm and she'll come around."

Devin punched me in the shoulder again. "What do you know about women, champ?"

I smiled, but said nothing.

Silence is golden.

I let her words hang in the ether like she'd committed a sin. While most peeps get uncomfortable with silence, I relished it. I twiddled my thumbs and the Uber driver's music got louder and Henri started licking the glass.

Twenty seconds later, she caved.

"Maybe cauliflower crust would be good."

The driver smiled. "Bacon and sausage it is."

He reached his right fist back over the seat and I fist-bumped it. Henri thought it was some sort of game, so he hit the dude's fist with his snout. We did another round of the game and that was that.

Then we were back to the road and the mundanities of travel. Objects whirled past and Henri barked and I nodded off and Devin tapped her foot to some pop songs on the driver's radio. It went like that until we were off the highway and waiting at the light off one of the exit ramps.

The driver was saying something about the Texans' quarterback woes, and I was just about to opine when we got rear-ended.

Henri squealed, and the driver swore like a sailor.

"Ain't this lovely," Devin said.

The impact was minimal, but the damage had been done. Police reports would be made and information exchanged and our quest to the van's address delayed.

"Some punk-ass kid," I said.

I pointed to the figure that had gotten out of the car. The kid looked no older than twenty, with earrings and headphones and a wifebeater undergarment.

"Oy vey," she said.

The driver got out of the car, and for a second Henri jumped onto the driver's seat and tried to join him, but I reined him in. The driver closed his door and Henri slinked back to his spot.

Devin smiled and moved closer to me.

"Thanks again for helping me out here. I imagine a champ has more important things on the itinerary when attempting to avoid camp."

"A champ's itinerary is malleable, missy."

She laughed, and that's when we heard the driver raise his voice. We both looked out the back of the window and saw the driver gesticulating with his hands. The kid was playing dumb.

He tried to hand the driver a piece of paper, but the driver kept pushing it back to him, asking for his insurance card. It went like this a few times, and then the kid had had enough. He threw the paper at the driver and stormed off. He revved his engine and a plume of dust enveloped our car.

The dust cleared, and the driver opened the door, fuming. Nothing like a hit-and-run in the Lone Star State.

"That fucking asshole. Gonna mess up my insurance, and my star rating."

"This is a five-star ride as far as I'm concerned," Devin said.

"Ditto," I said.

The driver took out his phone and called the police. And we waited. Henri barked at one of the cars veering around us in traffic. He'd spotted a beagle. Devin started biting her nails again, and I started tapping my foot to an even newer pop song on the radio.

"The asshole kept trying to write his info on some scratch paper," the driver said. "I ain't falling for those games. Been on these roads too long. Seen it all."

I nodded, but my curiosity got the better of me.

"Let me see it," I said. "Maybe it's legit."

The driver took the piece of paper out of his pocket and tossed it back to me. I was expecting chicken scratch and some LLC name nobody had ever heard of.

I got neither.

When I looked at the paper, there was a message on it.

For me and Devin.

And it was crystal clear.

The paper said, *Keep playing detective and we slit Jakey's throat.*

7

The trooper showed up seven minutes later. He wore khaki head to toe, a cowboy hat, aqua blue tie, and various epaulets I couldn't quite place. The hombre was a solid thirty-five pounds overweight and was chewing a big ole wad of gum. He cinched his belt as he talked and kept rearranging his hat. I wondered if they gave complimentary hats at the academy because he looked like he'd worn through many a pair.

The trooper took out a notepad from his breast pocket, but it was all perfunctory. He was a veteran of the badge, and he was agitated that he had to respond to a minor fender bender.

Henri and I stood on the sidewalk taking it all in. The Uber driver was giving his version of events and Devin was next to him chiming in when necessary. With each point of emphasis, the trooper nodded like he gave a shit, but he only selectively took notes. I wanted to march right up and examine his penmanship, but I let it be.

I still had the threatening message in my pocket. I took it out, read it again, and crumpled it back up. Games made the world go round, and I was eager to play this notemaker's game. One step closer to Jake.

Earlier, Devin had tossed the note back at me faster than you could say note. She was past intimidation and her resolve was even more steely. She knew Jake was still alive. The note confirmed it. The captors wanted something, and they knew that in order to get it they needed the collateral. Jake was the collateral. She felt it in her bones, and the whole dog-and-pony show didn't faze her one bit. The more she displayed it the more I digged her.

She didn't scare easily.

Bottom line, it'd be hell to pay for the notegiver-kidnapper extraordinaire. Once I found the culprit I'd be a gentleman and give Devin dibs on the first punch. Then it'd be a fight game master class. I'd give floating uppercuts and she'd give a mean guillotine. It'd go like that till we beat the gamer to a bloody pulp. There were no rounds on the street and there were no referees.

Just bring it.

Mess with family and you get the fucking horns.

Henri started whining, so I pulled out a biscuit. The Uber driver had some for his dog-carrying customers and had given me a handful for the road. He saved me a trip to the local pet place, and he definitely was getting a five-star review when this show concluded. Henri had other plans though. He sniffed the biscuit and turned away. He was used to grain-free healthy varieties, and he'd snuffed this one out. Regular dog fare. Mass production.

But I was one step ahead of Henri sometimes. I tossed the biscuit around in my hands and made airplane noises with it. Henri must have thought the biscuit had transformed because he grabbed it out of my hands, lay down on the ground, and took his time with every morsel. When he was done I rubbed the top of his head and Henri stood watch over the accident scene.

The traffic pattern had corrected itself now that the Uber driver's car and the trooper's were on the shoulder. The wind was coming from the east and the temps were just starting to creep into the high eighties. Even though I held a general disdain for the blue given my past, if I had a medal I'd give it to the trooper for sheer ability to withstand the humidity in all his getup. The hat itself had minimal breathability.

Devin walked over to me and rubbed Henri's belly. He groaned, licked her hands, but stayed in roll call position. He was a good boy.

"The cop's gonna talk to you next," she said.

"I welcome the governmental intrusion."

She rolled her eyes and we started talking more about Jake and next steps. We made sure to keep our voices down so the trooper wouldn't interfere in our investigation. I wanted to still go to the address the van was registered to. Devin didn't want to stir the pot and thought it was a dead end. She wanted to wait for more texts from the damned notemaker. We talked for a few minutes, going in circles at times and making novel proposals at others. At the end of it all I was chivalrous and agreed to table the address chase. If the notemaker was fond of texting games, then more clues were afoot.

We started talking about random shit, and I was laughing at one of her jokes when the trooper finally walked over to me.

"Look what the cat dragged in," the trooper said. He snarled his nose and furrowed his brows. He rearranged his hat again.

I was used to getting lukewarm reactions from the blue all across the nation. Perhaps it had to do with the fact that I bashed people's brains in for a living—or the fact that I'd done twelve years for a murder I didn't commit and many in blue still held the belief that I was guilty as all hell and got off because of some slick lawyering.

Or perhaps they just didn't like my fashion. I wore slim-cut everything and always color-coordinated.

I had a retort at the ready.

"That's an interesting aqua tie," I said.

The trooper looked down at his tie and tidied it for a second. "What's it to you, son?"

"I enjoy lighter hues, but a knockoff's a knockoff. You can't pull a fast one on me, Deputy."

He scrunched his nose and flipped a new leaf on his notepad.

"Did you see the man who caused this here accident?"

"Seeing and sharing are completely different entities," I said.

I flashed my pearly whites. The trooper didn't return the gesture. He started scribbling on his notepad. From my vantage point it looked aesthetic more than anything else, but I'd learned long ago never to doubt the pad. People's lives were made and destroyed by that pad, and judges relied on testimony based off that pad.

The deputy looked up.

"Lookee here, Gedrin. Everybody has a job to do. I knew you would be a pain in my ass the minute you got here. You think I don't know when a famous murderer comes to this town? You've been all over the fucking airwaves since yesterday. My job is to make sure that the riff-raff stays *out* of this here town. Property values and taxes and all that shit depend on it. You understand?"

I nodded. "Funding is muy bueno."

"What the hell did you see?"

"A punk-ass kid with headphones."

"Any other distinguishing features?"

"Left earring. Silver. Right earring I couldn't tell."

"Did he say anything to you?"

"Absolutely nada," I said. "I was guarding this monster here."

The trooper looked down at Henri, who ignored the trooper. His master had taught him the importance of pleading the fifth.

"Well, I reckon this matter will best be handled by the insurance powers that be."

I agreed, but I didn't share the sentiment aloud. I stood there holding Henri's leash with a less than amused expression.

"Zoom or in person?" I said.

"What now?" the trooper asked.

"Court. Is this poor Uber man supposed to go down to the courthouse to prosecute this case, or is it all on the computer?" Society was trending more toward video for everything, and I'd heard that the courts were forced to follow suit despite their archaic ways.

The trooper snorted. "It's all fucking Zoom. Now these pieces of shit can get out of bed, open their phones, and start making excuses to the damned judge with a bad internet connection. Lot of scammers on there too."

"May the excuses be ever in their favor," I said.

"Gedrin, you're a piece of work, you know that?"

"You won't be the first and you won't be the last to tell me that, Deputy. Sir."

The trooper scribbled some more shit on his notepad and then ripped off one of the pages.

"Give this to the driver. My sciatica is killing me this morning and I'm not gonna take any more unnecessary steps today."

He started walking back toward his car.

I smiled. "Sorry, can't. I would prefer no liability in case he misses court and the case gets dropped against his behest."

The trooper turned and winced, holding his back. "Fucking Gedrin. You should have lost to Golota, but the ref gave you a long count."

Golota was my first title fight and it had ruffled a lot of feathers. I didn't remember any long counts or any knockdowns. But I guess others did. Such was the name of the game.

The trooper swiped the paper out of my hand, walked to the Uber driver, and handed it to him. The driver palmed it, nodded, and continued his conversation on the phone.

Then the trooper came back over to me and cinched his belt one last time.

"Look here, Gedrin. I'm not the type to hold a grudge. But your reputation precedes you. No bullshit here. I've got friends in Chicago. Let me give you one last piece of advice. No matter how many fucking pussies you knock out and how much dirty money you get, you'll always be looking over your shoulder in this town. Texas is built different, son. If you're thinking of causing a ruckus, you best stop now before things go south. Lots of powerful people out in these parts."

He emphasized the *powerful people* part, and then just like that he was gone. He hopped in his squad car, turned off his oscillating lights, and burned rubber.

The trooper did me a solid.

I never got arrested in Texas.

8

Before the investigation continued, I had to drop off Henri at doggy daycare. Henri was the quintessential service companion, but sometimes he presented an impediment to solving my latest mystery. For starters, there was no way I could house enough biscuits in my pocket to assuage his appetite, and he was such a furball that my allergies flared up when his coat wasn't getting the right amount of TLC.

So Devin found a daycare/grooming place on the outskirts of San Antonio, and I took Henri in at about half past noon. The place wasn't the Ritz by any means, but it had a large play area with adequate stimulation for all canine shapes and sizes. All told, about nine canines were currently romping about, including two shih tzus who were having a blast going up and down a ramp in one corner. They did at least seven loops on the ramp, hopped over a bloodhound that was asleep nearby, then went back and poked at him until he woke up and joined the ramp party, albeit with far less zeal than his shih tzu companions. In another corner were toys in various states of disrepair—ropes, tennis balls, Kong toys with treats. Several kibble bowls were spread out in triangular patterns, and leashes hung on the wall in front of the bowls.

Henri normally loved these opportunities to meet new furry friends. He'd abandon all leash manners and let everybody know he was the new sheriff in town. But this time he was pulling the opposite way on the leash to get the hell outta Dodge.

He knew what was up. A dog's intuition is second to none. He'd be abandoned for a stretch, and he'd be forced to make do with the shih tzus. He'd never seen eye to eye with shih tzus.

A cheery front desk girl broke my rhythm. "Reservation, sir?"

"Yes, under Henri the incredible," I said.

The girl started typing on her computer, then stopped. "I'm sorry, we don't have that one here."

"Lo siento. What's the daily rate?" I said.

The girl was flustered for a second, then she realized I was playing her. She told me the rate and tried to sell me packages of stays, but I politely informed her of my nomad status. I included all the pertinent parts and left out all the others. Since I was getting a grooming in addition to the one play session, she reduced the daily rate by a few dollars and threw in a complimentary FURminator brushing.

Satisfied, I handed her Henri's leash.

She stuck her palm out. "Just a few intake questions before we handle your loved one."

"By all means," I said.

Devin punched me in the shoulder, and that made a plethora of punches for the day. Things were solid between us.

"Any allergies?" the cheery girl said.

"Kibble is a no-go," I said.

"What does he eat?"

"Raw food and grain-free treats from time to time. The occasional off-the-shelf biscuit if he's not being picky."

"That's expensive," the girl said.

"Family is family."

She smiled.

After I'd adopted Henri, I made Sims put a clause in my fight contracts stating that his company would pay for all incidentals incurred during camp—including any and all sustenance for Henri, along with his toys, groomings, plays, leashes, harnesses, crates, t-shirts, shit bags, and more. With Sims picking up the tab, Henri was living like a king, and I swiped my credit card so often I routinely got carpal tunnel. I had no qualms at all. Sims got to write it all off on his taxes for business purposes. Shysters and commerce made proper bedfellows.

"When did he last eat?" the girl asked.

"About six and a quarter hours ago at one of the finest motels in town."

The girl laughed and looked at her computer again. "Temperament?"

"Optimistic."

"How is he with other dogs?"

"He's a wildcard to be honest. Those shih tzus over there should get off those ramps. The hound is a candidate for best friend status. The others are in wait-and-see mode. If he senses they aren't genuine in any way, it's game over. If they have good character, then he may join multiple cliques today."

The girl was flustered as she typed in my responses. She asked a few more questions—about Henri's shitting habits, drinking habits, nails, and fur—and that's all she wrote. She took Henri's leash, Devin rubbed his whiskers, and I told Henri I'd be back in no time. He looked at me like I had committed the ultimate betrayal, then he ignored me and sauntered off into the play area.

"We close at six," the girl said.

"Indeed," I said.

Devin and I walked out, and Sims must have telepathically channeled his inner fur parent because he called right at that moment.

"I have three new gray hairs this fucking morning," he said. "How many times have I told you to keep that damned Jitterbug charged? I have new merchandising and trademark opportunities for your next fight."

I put Sims on speaker for entertainment purposes. Devin and I took a seat on a bench near the parking lot.

"My data is slow," I said.

"You're on fucking unlimited."

"Maybe I need a fruit phone."

Sims ignored the comment and got right down to business.

"You wear some LED shorts with some cereal shit on it and you get half a mill."

"I'm gonna wear that maple syrup t-shirt and they can shove it up their asses," I said.

"Dammit, listen for once."

Sims gave me the full scoop on the opportunities. I listened quite seriously for a bit, then I tuned him out. I always did. I just wanted to kick some ass on my terms. Sponsors and all be damned.

When we were through discussing the merits, Sims said, "And Sal set camp. Devil's Door. The ferry leaves first thing Monday morning. He has the tickets, and you better be on fucking time for once."

Devin laughed, and that's when Sims picked up on it.

"Eavesdropping are we, my lady?"

"I have a potential client for ya," I said.

Sims went quiet.

Then I told him about Devin.

Sims didn't miss a beat.

"You would have still been on the main card if you were a straw weight," he said to Devin. "Divison is flat as fuck and in need of some star power. Why you went up is beyond me."

"Fuck you," Devin said.

"I like her already," Sims said. "You're on the consideration list."

I ended the shysterfest. "You can tell Sal that unless I solve my latest sleuth, the ferry can leave without me."

Sims cursed a million words under the sun.

"Anton Tens," Devin said. "The fucker had my brother kidnapped and it's gonna be hell to pay when I find him."

"You really can pick 'em," Sims said.

The line went quiet again for a beat.

"He was always a greedy fuck," Sims said. "He tried to corner the boxing game, but I wouldn't let him. That's why he had a stable of MMA fighters. The pay isn't the same and the fighters get fucking taken advantage of by the promoters. He saw a window and he took it. Repped a lot of peeps, but did he really rep them? That's the thing."

Devin nodded as Sims was talking.

"I often ask whether you rep me fully," I said. "The jury's still out."

I laughed, and Sims did too. The agent-client relationship is an interesting one. Sims and I had our ups and downs, but definitely more ups than downs. And it appeared he was here to stay and be my champion. So I'd ride with him till the very end and make the asshole some money in the process. And I'd be a pain in the ass whenever my heart desired.

"There's a fourth gray hair. What's the damage this time?"

"For what?"

"Your latest splurge. And don't tell me nada. I can read you like the back of my fucking hand, Gedrin."

I thought about some funny retort, but I was blanking. "Your nephew is getting his nails clipped and he's making friends with the hounds."

"You're lucky I like him. Just keep the receipts," Sims said.

"Gracias. Now where can we find Tens? I wanna give him a piece of my mind."

"Don't even think about it, Gedrin. Let the cops handle it. They have all these task forces for that kinda shit. And you don't want to be interfering in an investigation. Again. When are you ever gonna learn?"

"I'll learn when justice is served."

"Well, it may already have been," Sims said. "Tens croaked last week. Heart attack. It made some of the local papers out there. Guess he never laid off the cheeseburgers. The fat ass."

"Who was with him?" I said.

"Fuck if I know," Sims said. "Probably some side piece. Let it be."

"No can do, hombre."

I hung up.

Devin smiled.

"Anton always kept his side pieces local," she said. "How convenient."

She gave me the scoop, and we left the lot.

9

M andy's Pub sat on Crockett Street in the heart of San Antonio and had held the crown of swankiest piano bar for two decades running. Devin had been there on many a trip to Texas, and apparently one of Tens's old flames had an even bigger connection there.

She owned the place.

When Devin and I walked in, the place was two thirds empty, and there wasn't a hostess in sight. Crummy canvases lined the walls, the paint several years out of style. Grease wafted out of the kitchen, and some old blues tunes blared out of the jukebox. It was just past two in the afternoon, so the whole fare was par for the course.

We found a booth and took some menus. Even though it was lunch time, I still wanted breakfast. A breakfast of champions, since I'd worked up quite the appetite sleuthing all day. I scanned the menu for my favorite items, and I came up empty. Not a pancake, omelette, or hash brown in sight. Crepes were hiding too.

"Slim pickings," I said.

"They only serve lunch and dinner," Devin said.

"Breakfast is the most important meal of the day. Those who don't acknowledge its importance should be flogged."

"Complain to Poppy about it."

Poppy had been Tens's lover for close to a decade. On the ride over Devin had given me all the details. Poppy had been a ring girl just shy of her twenty-first birthday when Tens showed up to a fight and got her number. When he first tried to get drinks with her, she ghosted him. But Tens persisted. He showed up to all the fights she was working, and each time he gave her something special. Petunias. Bracelets. Earrings. Then he flew her on a jet to Paris, and that's what did the trick. She joined Tens's lavish lifestyle, and everybody in Tens's circle turned a blind eye after that.

I didn't press Devin for more details because I knew that story better than my own hand. I'd seen it from the very moment I turned pro. Infidelity was part and parcel of the celebrity game. All the famous peeps had side pieces and everybody in the inner circle knew not to say anything about those side pieces. Pretend they don't exist, and if the situation ever becomes too untenable, deny, deny, deny. Issue mercurial press releases and give circular talk. Dance around it like the best ballerina in town.

Silence is golden.

So Tens was banging Poppy and eventually the fling ran its course. Probably because wifey found out and disowned him. Simple as that.

"I'll start by telling her this upholstery is tragic," I said, pointing to the ripped pink hues around the booth.

"Classic never goes out of style," Devin said.

I agreed with her on that one, so I let it be. A waiter eventually showed up and took our orders. I settled for a cheeseburger on a poppy bun with steak fries, while Devin got a chicken salad.

"Some camp," Devin said.

"Calorie expenditure is the name of the game right now. I overconsume and then finely cut. Like a fine onion mincing."

Devin laughed and moved a little closer to me in the booth. Despite the circumstances of the day it seemed that things were building between us. I'd be lying if I said I objected to that, but then again I'd be lying if I said I wanted that buildup. My head wasn't exactly the most stable, my habits weren't really changing, and I had no idea what I wanted in the love department. But I figured it would hit me in the head one day, and like Edison and the lightbulb there'd be no way back. For now, a lack of clarity was soothing indeed.

We talked about random shit for a few minutes, and then our food came. We really had the connects, because Poppy delivered our meals personally.

"Chicken salad for the princess and big hearty for the champ," Poppy said. She set our plates down and gave me a ketchup bottle. The squeeze kind.

Devin got up and hugged her and Poppy plopped down in the booth next to us. She looked a weathered thirty-five, but she radiated beauty and new money and sex. I could see why Tens had fallen for her. A blonde bombshell with perfect pearly whites and a business acumen to boot. She checked the boxes and had probably left a trail of scorned suitors in her wake.

"Long time no see, cutie," Poppy said.

"Been hustling," Devin said.

"'Bout time you quit that old thing. That pretty face of yours doesn't need any more punches now, does it? I've been too up close and personal with all that nonsense, and I don't want to see you not get up next time."

"Thanks, Poppy."

They shared a laugh while I doused ketchup over my fries. The bottle produced asymmetric squeezed portions, but I persisted one chunk at a time. At one point I closed the cap and started smacking the back for even more.

"That's our last bottle till corporate comes tomorrow," Poppy said. "Easy does it."

I managed to get the right amount of ketchup out, then placed the bottle at the center of the table by the napkin holder.

"The champ isn't exactly a great influence," Devin said.

Poppy smiled. "Two's always better company," she said. "Especially the athletic kind."

She looked me up and down seductively for a second. Then she turned her gaze around to some of the other tables, summoned a waiter and gave him constructive criticism, and hollered at a busboy. When she was done roasting, she turned her attention back to us.

"So what brings you two out here on a fine summer afternoon?"

I considered blurting it all out, but I held back. Poppy needed to think she was in control. Then I would get the job done.

"For the pancakes," I said. "But the upholstery needs work." I pointed at the rough spots on the booth.

"Corporate is stalling on that too, my friend. The workers don't wanna work much these days with this heat. The pancakes are up for debate. Might bring in more customers, but way more overhead."

"You can't go wrong with the most important meal of the day," I said.

Devin poked me in the shoulder. She looked like she was about to spill, and I let her have at it.

"Somebody took Jake," she said.

49

Poppy gripped the table hard. "Who? Did you call the deputies?"

"They're the finest assholes I know. Cowboy hat or no," I said.

Devin rolled her eyes. "Anton is connected to it," she said.

Poppy looked like she'd seen a ghost. Then she leaned back in the booth and shook her head.

"It adds up," she said. "I haven't seen that fucker for years though. Not sure how much help I can be."

"You see him croak?" I said.

"Hell no. I heard from a friend of a friend. And I hate to say it, karma and all, but good. That man never played his cards straight. Always playing games and trying the next swindle. If all the people he fucked weren't gonna get to him, then something was."

"Who did he fuck?" I said.

Poppy rubbed her temples, and in that moment her eyes relived the decade spent with Tens. I saw a woman scorned and a love that was very much one-sided till the very end. That's how it usually went with celeb dalliances. Once the richer and more famous of the pair had had his or her fill of the fun, the parting of the ways was acrimonious to say the least.

She leaned into the table, then back against the booth. Then back into the table.

"Champ, you want the red pill or the blue pill?"

I loved film references. They brought me back to more blissful times, and they tested my brain cells.

She was talking about the Matrix. The Matrix is everywhere. Take the blue pill and you wake up in your bed. Total ignorance. Take the red pill and I show you how deep the rabbit hole goes.

Hell yeah.

"Red pill," I said.

Poppy looked around the bar again before turning back to me.

"Anton paid a hell of a lot to play."

10

"Pillow talk is real," Poppy said. "You fuck a man right and he starts singing like all the mockingbirds on a bright Sunday morning."

She reached over to my plate and stole one of my fries. When she tossed it in her mouth she made a face like the cooks had messed with the recipe, but then she smiled and took another.

"Anton would sing better than Sinatra. His business model was quite simple: build with the best and brightest and reap the rewards when they go pro. Shoes. Commercials. Bling. T-shirts. You name it, Anton was all over it. Stream City. That's what he called it. The more income streams, the more he could line his pocket, and the more he could absorb the athletes that flamed out. But he needed a leg up on the competition. Anybody with half a brain has multiple ways for clients to make money. Enter the boosters."

"Crooks," I said.

I'd had more than my fair share of slimeballs promising me everything under the sun to get me to turn pro. From fancy

Escalades to orgies to the latest kicks, they had no shame. Sims won the race back then, but his intentions were only slightly purer than the rest.

"Anton never recruited talent before high school," Poppy said. "Too young to earn. He started with the superstar high school freshmen and worked his way up from there. He couldn't pay high schoolers directly, but the boosters swooped in and got the Rolls and the Hummers and money for Momma to pay rent and utilities. And once the stars declared and made it to big boy campus, the boosters threw the dopest parties. Hooker central."

Devin rolled her eyes while I visualized the collegiate experience.

Poppy took another fry. "But the NCAA has rules. The stars needed to perform in the classroom too. Maybe not too much, but still. Minimums needed to be met or Anton would lose his future cash cows. He was counting the damned clock and buttering them up for the minute they turned pro. It was his own pipeline of green. One year for the basketball players, three for the footballers, and the MMA he sort of fell into, but not even one year of school for them. Fighters start super young. He paid off the profs to pass the players. He was a snake charmer, that's for sure. Most went along with the green. Hell, some even made up classes and syllabi and got the schools to accredit them. 'Basketball Origins' or 'Football History.' Bullshit."

Poppy turned from the table again to shout at one of the busboys, then was right back with us.

"But there're always lone wolves," she said. "They go against the grain. Neither Anton nor the boosters could buy their solidarity. Enter the runners."

I was having trouble seeing the picture painted by her spiel, but I'd learned long ago that there's two sides to every story. Be patient and good things will come. I finished my burger and played around with the remaining fries.

"They were nerds," Poppy said. "If the ballers were the best and brightest on the field, the nerds were the same in the class-room. They'd come in and audit the classes of the problem professors. The sticklers. The nerds would do the athletes' homework, angle their papers a certain way to let the athletes cheat off them, exchange answers in the stalls, even fucking cause a scene in the classroom if that's what it took to get the answers to the players. But they weren't always the *right* answers. If all the players started acing every test it'd be too fishy. So some athletes passed just barely, some with flying colors, and everything in between. The runners controlled it all. They were paper boys, but they got the players in the arena —and then the money came flowing in like Niagara Falls. The runners made Anton. But then they destroyed him."

Poppy went for another one of my fries, but they were all gone. She laughed.

"While Anton was singing to me, the runners were singing to the feds. They launched a years-long investigation into the cheating ring. And when your back is up against the wall, you know how it goes, champ."

Poppy raised her eyebrows at me, and it started clicking. Nobody liked a snitch. Especially in the courtroom. But when you're facing life and bologna sandwiches and non-peaceful showers and shanks it was easy to see how people caved. The biggest scumbags on earth went down because of some of these snitches. Sometimes innocents got caught up in the fray, too. But Anton was far from innocent.

I pieced it all together in my head, but I waited for Poppy to confirm it.

"They were facing big time in federal custody," she said, "and not the plushy work camp the politicians go to. The runners sang, and the case was readied for court. It stalled on some technicality and never got there. But I've heard rumblings that they're ready to bring it back."

Devin had been quiet this whole time. She hadn't pieced the puzzle together like I had. She was gripping the table hard, and for a moment I thought it was going to come right off the screws.

"Sorry, Poppy," she said. "But what the hell does this have to do with finding my brother?"

Poppy put a hand on her shoulder.

"Honey, Jake was a runner. He was one of Anton's best. And he was the first to snitch. He was the glue for the whole case. Sounds like they intercepted him right before court comes calling."

One of the benefits of beating people's brains in for a living is that I excel at reading body language. When someone wants to throw a punch, fake a punch, block a punch, rush the ring, choke somebody out, they telegraph it, and I can read it and act accordingly. The body doesn't lie.

Devin wanted to beat the shit out of Poppy. Her jaw tightened and the corner of her lip curled upward. Her traps got bigger. I was expecting a quick jab and that'd be all she wrote. I waited for it. "Nothing I could do to stop this man's operation, honey," Poppy said. "I was just along for the ride like everybody else."

Devin relented and stayed quiet. I was impressed.

"Sorry you're going through all this honey," Poppy said. "Anton was a piece of shit." She put a hand on Devin's shoulder and pulled her in for a hug. She allowed it.

"Anton's dead. So who the hell took the kid?" I said.

"My bet's on the Silver Saints. The biggest motorcycle gang in town. Anton paid them to give protection to his best players and keep them out of trouble. The athletes never had to worry about people extorting them for money or robbing them or none of that because of the muscle on the payroll."

It added up. If my experience in court had taught me anything, it was that witnesses and gangbangers did not mix. No face, no case. If the Saints were implicated, they would make damned sure that Jake wasn't gonna testify—or any runner for that matter. They'd threaten them all and make them recant, or simply not show up to court when it mattered. But it might not have been necessary; if the feds had been building a case for years and still hadn't indicted anybody, it was probably all smoke and mirrors. The feds were just hoping to strike lightning in a bottle. But the criminals were one step ahead. No runners, no case. Of course, that still left Anton. I was willing to bet the Saints had made him croak too.

Self-preservation is a beautiful thing.

"Where can I find them?" I said.

Poppy looked around the bar again before gazing back at me. "They're sprinkled in every dive bar around this great state of Texas. Can't miss the Harleys."

"How many?"

"Five thousand strong."

With those numbers I'd have better luck playing scratch golf back in New Mexico.

"You want answers? Go straight to the source," she said. "Anton's biggest players. They know the bigwig Saints."

"We aren't in Tinseltown," I said. "The stars that live out here wanna be off the grid."

Poppy nodded.

But Devin spoke up.

"I know a quarterback who never left home. Anton wouldn't shut the fuck up about him."

11

Lyle Tam was synonymous with perfection. From the time he picked up a pair of football cleats in the sixth grade, he was a winner. He started at wide receiver, but after he threw a few perfect spirals on some trick plays, his coaches switched him to quarterback. He'd never looked back.

Tam made varsity his freshman year, and his team won state the next four seasons. When he declared for UT, the naysayers were ready to see him decimated by the competition. He gave them plenty of fodder. An ankle injury suffered in practice lingered, and he sat out his first few games. Then he pulled a hamstring in warmups and sat out a few more games. But when he was finally healthy and the reins were handed to him, he was all that and then some. UT dominated the competition and made a bowl game every year with Tam under center. He rarely lost a game, and when he declared for the NFL, he was slated to be the first quarterback picked in the draft. He shot up everybody's draft board and was the consensus number one pick. Sponsors lined up around the block to get Tam to rep the latest gadgets. He had the look and the game of a superstar. Bottom line, he had the "it" factor, and everybody knew it.

But just like boxing, in football, one shot can end it all.

Tam blew out his knee on Senior Day running the option, and he never recovered. Tam underwent multiple reconstructive surgeries and missed the combine. No NFL team wanted to risk draft capital on a player that was reported to be a good two years out from ever seeing the field again. Tam eventually healed up, but he was never quite right after that. He landed on some NFL practice squads, but found himself outplayed and outmatched. He was never signed to a team's roster. At the end of the day winning was everything.

Tam's football journey ended on a fall day a few years after he blew out his knee, and he never picked up the cleats again. He did some play-by-play for UT games for a while, and last anybody heard he was running summer camps for quarterbacks, which yielded some dividends as well as publicity for the former star.

I was flabbergasted by Devin's knowledge of Tam's history. If I was the professor on the inside, she was the dean, because her encyclopedia of sports history trumped mine any day of the week.

But what was important was her belief that Tam knew the Saints—and that he would give us the scoop on Jake. I wholeheartedly agreed. Tam had as much clout as anybody in the Lone Star State, and where there was clout there was bound to be muscle. Getting closer to the Saints meant getting closer to finding Jake.

I couldn't say I was surprised to learn that Jake had been running for Anton. On the surface he might have seemed an innocent kid, but I'd learned over the years that appearances can be quite deceiving. My time at Pontiac had taught me to never judge a book by its cover. The tamest, skinniest hombres oftentimes were the ones that could cut your throat the quickest. Their true colors were fucking ruthless. Always sleep with your eyes open.

So even as we looked for Jake, I knew deep down that he would be able to suck it up and hold his own. He was smart, if he was running. He was more sophisticated than met the eye. Knowledge is power, and the kid had leverage with his testimony. He'd probably figured out by now that he could dangle it like a carrot over his captors to stay alive.

Keep it up, Jake.

The Uber dropped us off in Champions Ridge. Devin had done some social media sleuthing on Tam's location, and the results had pointed us to this exclusive gated community outside San Antonio.

When we walked up to the gate, the security guard recognized us right away, but he wouldn't let us through. I figured a selfie might grant us entry, but honesty really is the best policy sometimes. I told him we were there to see Tam.

The guard furrowed his brows for a second, then he stepped back into the security booth and flipped through a booklet. The Rolodex of rich denizens of the ridge must have been long, because it took him a while to find the right place. He ran his finger down the names, and when he eventually found his mark he made the call. A half minute later, he smiled and opened the gate.

Devin and I walked inside, and I was struck by the majesty of the place. Four-thousand-square-foot residences were the norm here. They had pristine lawns and porches and scenic canyon views. Tens had probably had a plethora of these residences in his heyday, but some good that did him. There was no escaping your expiration date.

"Second house at the top," Devin said. She was looking at her phone's GPS.

"I'll take the third from the top."

It appeared to be the smallest of the ones we'd seen thus far and it had an eccentric design to it.

"Stop it."

"Say it like you mean it."

"Stop it."

She looked me in the eye and I held her gaze for an eternity. We stood there in the middle of the roadway lost in it all. A car rounded the bend and almost sideswiped us, but I didn't care. The situation called for only one thing.

Nature.

Let it run its course.

I pulled her close and kissed her. She enjoyed it and wrapped her arms around my neck and asked for more. We stood there for who the hell knows how long caressing each other's lips and laughing at nothing in particular.

Then we were spotted.

"The champ is here!" a voice said.

I broke from Devin and saw a tall black dude in green basketball shorts coming toward us. He had pythons for arms and tats running all over his shoulders. He looked like he could still run a solid forty time, even at his age, which I pegged as late thirties.

This had to be Tam.

He stopped in front of me and sized me up. He started at my quads and went up to my traps before staring at my arms, then his. I was always ready to throw down if need be, but the hombre seemed friendlier than most.

He put his hand out.

"Lyle. Sims used to rep me back in the day. I hear he's still on top."

That shyster. I shook anyway.

"Sims will never cede his crown."

Tam laughed.

Devin shook his hand too, and he recognized her.

"Two undisputeds! What brings y'all out here?"

I gave a circular answer that didn't quite get to the heart of the matter, and Tam bought it.

"Come inside and have a drink," he said. "It's the least I could do for the two of you. Not often we get champs up here on the ridge."

I smiled.

We were getting closer to the Saints.

12

The camps paid well. When Tam opened his front door we were led into a foyer with a fifteen-foot ceiling and huge atrium windows that brought wide swaths of sunlight flooding in. On one wall a solid oak end table was perched under a full-length mirror, and on the opposite wall hung a canvas of an opera singer, her tongue stretching for several feet. The canvas was part vintage, part street style with yellow graffiti covering the corners and classic block lettering in the center. I wasn't good with musical periods, so I didn't even try to date the piece.

Tam checked himself out in the mirror, rolling his green shorts up and down to showcase the striations in his quads before trudging on to the living room. Devin took the mirror next, inspecting her shoulder blades. When I passed the mirror I pretended I was invisible. I'd shed any and all excess calories at camp. If Sal did his job, I'd be cut up for the fight. After all, that's what the senile hombre was getting paid the big bucks for. Leaner and meaner.

As I walked into the living room I almost got bowled over

by a Cane Corso. He was gray brindle with bowling balls for paws. He smelled me for several seconds, then pushed me back with his snout and got down on all fours, wagging his tail so fast I thought he was gonna knock all the furniture down.

"Leslie, leave it," Tam said.

The dog shook his head.

"Wifey always wanted a dog because she was deprived as a child, but then we went ahead and adopted the biggest one in the shelter. Leslie still doesn't understand that humans don't enjoy a one-hundred-fifty-pound hug all the time."

"Go big or go home," I said.

"His shits are bigger than mine," Tam said.

"My boy's playing with a bloodhound." I told Tam about Henri—nutrition, obedience, and beyond. Tam nodded at all the right times and laughed at all the others. He'd been trained well by Sims. The art of looking like you're giving a fuck while not actually giving a fuck. Media Relations 101. No wonder the shyster got the big bucks.

While we were talking about our canines, Devin stood by a couch overlooking a patio. It was another expansive space, and Tam's pool glistened in the distance—a custom build-out with a diving board to boot. I pictured Leslie doing cannonballs off the top and giving the cleaning crew quite the surprises at the bottom.

"Water, tea?" Tam said.

He walked to the opposite side of a kitchen island, opened up one of the cabinets, and pulled out glasses.

"Can't go wrong with aqua pura," I said.

"Weak shit," Tam said. "Whisky makes me most productive."

He smiled, then poured himself a glass from a bottle on the counter. He held it up for Devin, but she shook her head.

"I'm good," she said.

He took another glass, went to the fridge, and poured me some water.

I took it and chugged it in record time. While I generally wanted to avoid any thoughts on camp till I got there, hydration was a whole other matter. I needed to drink to keep my headaches at bay and feel fully on the ball. I'd piss it all out in short order, but without hydration all sorts of problems cropped up for a brain basher: dry skin, fever, delirium. I drank away and went through a minimum of twelve cups a day.

I noticed that Devin had a hint of a frown on her face. She didn't make eye contact with me, and she kept staring out at the pool. When Leslie went over to her, she ignored him, and the big guy went over to his bed in the corner and started napping. One of the many reasons I'd never had success with the female sex was that I couldn't quite read the room. A few minutes ago Devin and I were thick as thieves, on a mission to find the kid. Seductive gazes. Lips dancing together. Minds free and clear. Now she was giving me the silent treatment. No bueno.

But luckily for me, I had a plan that by and large got the job done in these types of situations. I'd honed a strategy over the years that shifted the vibe in the room pronto. The more Devin wanted to shut me out, the more I would shut *her* out.

Silence on both ends.

That was the key.

Eventually the original silencer breaks. The average human avoids long periods of silence. It makes them feel awkward and uneasy and uncouth. I relished silence. If my twelve years in a cell had taught me anything positive, it was that one can live in luxury in his own mind. My city. My rules. My peace. Nothing else mattered.

I ignored Devin and kept my attention on Tam. "How long were you with that shyster Sims?"

Tam laughed. "When you're on top of the world, they're

coming at you every which way. Ethics don't mean shit, you feel me? Sims plucked me out of the crowd."

I nodded.

"But Sims seemed more true than the rest of the assholes," Tam continued. "He actually wanted me not just to make money, but to save it and build for a rainy day. He kept telling me this wouldn't all last. And he was right."

Sims did have some redeeming qualities. For one, he ate well and preached proper nutrition. For another, he truly put the pedal to the metal trying to find gigs for his clients—from signing caps and t-shirts, to gracing the covers of cereal boxes, to doing underwear ads. Sims's tenacity for his clients knew no bounds.

I let Tam keep running his mouth. He talked about the first deep ball he ever threw for a touchdown and his favorite coach and his Heisman trophy. This was all part of the plan. Get the subject to feel comfortable with your presence. Ease them along, and then go for the kill.

The reason I was here.

The fucking Saints. Where the hell were the shot callers hiding?

I sipped my water as Tam droned on about the groupie college girls that would follow him around on road games. He took another shot of whisky and described how some of the opposing cheerleaders joined the groupies and would take turns riding him before and after the games, unbeknownst to the coaching staff. This was all before the dawn of social media, and Tam kept emphasizing that fact. The more Tam talked, the more I could see how much he missed his old rock-star life.

Devin shook her head, her eyes remaining on the pool outside.

I smiled and still didn't make eye contact. She'd crack in no time. I walked to the opposite side of the island and took a seat on one of the bar stools.

"When did the asshole cut you?" I said.

I was referring to Sims, but Tam took a broader view.

"Once my knee had other plans, they knew. Everybody can see that shit. Everybody but you. I never felt springy after that. All the gyms and therapists in the world can't run for a first down or throw a forty-yard out route to the sideline for you." Tam leaned against the island and closed his eyes. "Now I'm shouting at wannabe Heisman kids that couldn't even fucking hold my strap. The parents are even worse. They talk shit about reps and playbooks. Damn, if your kid can't throw four thousands yards in prep, how they gonna do it at the next level?"

"Preach," I said.

Devin laughed, but still didn't look my way. I was getting close though.

Leslie rose from his nap, went over to Tam, and started begging.

"No. You had breakfast already," Tam said. "Two big breakfasts."

He gave some commands, but nada. Once a furry friend has other things on his mind it's game over.

"Duck works wonders," I said.

"What?"

"Biscuits," I said. I reached into my pocket and discovered a phantom duck biscuit left that I'd forgotten about. Poor Henri had been deprived of the good stuff.

I showed it to Tam. "Grain-free and some other shit on the packaging. It'll keep him full till chow time again."

Tam thought it over for a second, then caved. He nodded, and I lowered the treat toward Leslie's nose. The monster didn't sit right away, but I waited till I had his undivided attention.

He sat.

I waited.

I motioned my palm down.

Leslie stared at me for a few seconds, then got down on all fours and waited patiently.

"Fucking whisperer Gedrin over here," Tam said.

"That's how I roll," I said.

I gave Leslie the treat, and her jaw speed made Henri look like an amateur. I took another sip of my water, and decided it was time to go for the kill.

"I'm gonna be straight with you, hombre."

Tam nodded.

"Her brother's been kidnapped and we need the fucking scoop."

Tam's eyebrows shot up. "What? How? Go to the police. The troopers are good here."

"The khaki boys ain't gonna do shit, and you know that." My turn to size up Tam now. I stared him up and down. He had me by a max of seven pounds and had double my girth, but I liked it that way. It made me more elusive when throwing hands. I doubted he would be stupid enough to try, but always be ready to fight. They try you, you show them what's what.

Sal 101.

"The ones that gave you those fucking cars and necklaces and Timberlands. That's who I want."

Tam furrowed his brows.

"The Saints have him," I said.

Tam straightened up. "Get the hell outta here. Busting in here trying to get me mixed up in somebody else's business. I respect y'all, but best you be leaving before I make a call."

"You got the Saints on speed dial," I said.

He froze for a few seconds, and that's when I knew Poppy was right. The eyes never lie.

"I'm calling," he said. "Leave, bro. *Now!* I don't want no trouble." He came around the island, and I got up from my stool and sized him up from close range.

He stepped back.

Just what I thought.

Then Devin turned away from the window and broke her silence.

"He's the only brother I have, and he never had a chance after my mom died. He's autistic, and if they put another finger on him, I'm gonna kill them all, one by one."

She started crying.

If the silent treatment was a powerful tool in the woman's arsenal, the waterworks were even better.

I rolled with it.

"Fess up, junior," I said. "Before I take away your throwing hand." I clenched my fist and got closer to him.

But his eyes hardened.

"Motherfucker, I've dealt with scum like you my whole life. You don't have shit. You're shooting your shot and coming up empty, cuz."

"A name. Give me the shot caller's name. Now."

Devin cried harder.

Tam looked at me, then at Devin, then back at me again. The gears were churning in his head. He wanted to preserve himself, but he wanted to help too.

He caved. His eyes were the tell again.

"Mario Sofa. He runs the territory around here. Bad dude. I'm not shitting you. If he has your brother, he's as good as gone."

Devin collapsed to the floor. I helped her up and she sat on one of the stools.

"Where the fuck is he?" I said.

Then I heard sirens in the distance.

Not again.

Tam looked at us. "Sorry. I have a panic button for unprecedented situations. This is one of them."

He moved away from the island and I saw the small button.

"A man's gotta protect hisself at all times. Everybody's watching."

Self-preservation indeed.

I jumped over Leslie and got the hell outta Dodge.

13

Devin ran toward the back fence. I was a few steps behind. I grabbed the pool railing and catapulted myself forward to pick up speed, the sirens getting closer in the distance. But pride cometh before the fall. The cobblestone patio sharply dropped down to the grass, and I stepped wrong. I felt my knee buckle for a second, then I rolled down the grass like a complete amateur.

I bounced back up, gathered myself, and sprinted toward the fence. It was vinyl with plenty of rails on the back that could serve as footholds, so I easily hoisted myself up. I could hear Tam shouting in the background, but I ignored it. If I didn't get over the top maybe he'd release Leslie and that'd be the end of it.

Devin's right shoe got caught in one of the brackets near the top of the fence. She pulled it free and ripped her joggers in the process. I still believed in chivalry despite the silent treatment, so I waited patiently for her to get across. When she did, I launched myself over the fence to freedom.

Or so I thought.

The minute I got over, big-ass shrubs scraped my skin and loose branches made me roll both my ankles.

Devin had already paid the price.

"Fuck," she said.

"She speaks," I said.

I smiled, but Devin went silent again and kept running. I could still hear the sirens, but wasn't sure if they were real. Perhaps Tam had called them off and I was just experiencing PTSD again from all my prior encounters with those in blue. Even though I could do time standing on my head with my eyes closed spinning around like a yoyo, the visual of the dirty bars and the odor of shit and piss still fucked with me. The hair on the back of my head stood up and my body ran cold for a few seconds till I got my bearings.

We ran for several minutes straight with no route in mind. We found a gravelly pathway and followed its scissor-like meandering for miles. It seemed like an old railway area, as the farther we went the more we saw rusty bits of track and even some bits of old-school railcars too. Hell, some of them looked like they'd been placed there during the Texas Revolution.

The houses we passed now, on both sides, were less bougie, more middle tier. Small fillable pools. Small decks. Small grills. Small fences with no privacy. I slowed to a walk. I didn't want a random yard dweller to call in two running buffoons. Devin slowed too. We walked at this new pace for a while, taking in the birds and the bees and getting a heavy dose of sunburn.

Three minutes later she finally spoke to me.

"I'm sorry," she said.

"Cool," I said.

She didn't make eye contact with me, but two words were better than none. We kept walking and talking.

"I've never been good with these kinda things. It's been a long time, if you know what I mean."

"The love department is an interesting beast."

She laughed. "Yeah. People are always turned off by what I do. They think I'm gonna go all psycho on them one day or something. That I can't handle my emotions. That I'm manly and have no feminine in me. I can't help it if I'm good at beating people up and getting paid for it."

I slowed my walk some more.

"Getting paid for it is the cherry on top," I said. "Some hombres just never learn. Never let them label you, Devin. Not now, not ever. You got to where you are by fucking busting your ass and chasing the dream you've had from when you could barely put on shin pads or do your own wraps. To climb the mountain. You've been there, so you can do whatever the fuck you want. The love department doesn't define you."

"Thanks." Devin still wasn't making eye contact, but I was enjoying the conversation this way. It took a bit of the pressure off.

We picked up our pace.

"De nada," I said.

"Do you always say random Spanish words like that? My old trainer would be impressed. He taught me a few gems."

"A magician never reveals his secrets."

Devin smiled. "I don't want to rush into anything," she said. "But I don't want to be a booty call either. I want to spend time with someone I really enjoy spending time with. I want to feel the butterflies all over, all the time."

"That makes sense," I said.

At the end of the day we, as humans, all desire some sort of connection with another human. Whether platonic or romantic, fleeting or lasting, when two people share the same space, there's a dialogue that takes place. When both sides are on the same page, the dialogue is crisp and clean and seamless. It sings on the page and makes things muy bueno.

"You probably have women throwing themselves at you everywhere you go," Devin said. "I don't even wanna know how many. The champ. Off death row for something you didn't do. And a whole lot of zeros in that bank account too. Can't change that."

"I'd beat people's brains for free if Sims would allow it," I said.

"Good one, Gedrin."

I walked a little closer to Devin, but we still were walking parallel along the gravel path, not making eye contact.

She kicked at some gravel. "I just don't want to get hurt. A dude put a ring on it once, then took it back at the altar. Figures, right? The only one that put up with me figured me out and bailed."

"Shit."

I let the word hang, partly because I was genuinely surprised by her comment, but also because I didn't quite have a response. Hell hath no fury like a woman scorned, but a woman scorned at the altar? That was next-level scorn.

"It was a small ceremony with no cameras, but still. Fucker messed me up good. So I don't trust right now. Except for these." She clenched her fists. "You came into my life like a fucking storm and I'm all in my head about it."

I walked even closer to Devin, and she followed suit.

"I'm fine with platonic," I said. "Really."

Devin said nothing.

Then she turned toward me and smiled.

"You do have soft lips, champ."

"That's how I roll."

"But you smell."

"Like what?"

"A Poppy cheeseburger."

I laughed.

Devin put her hand out. I took it and we walked like that for a while, Devin recounting memories of her brother, me recounting memories of my mom. At times her thumb ran circles around my hand and she gripped me tighter. It went like that for several minutes, before Devin went back to fighting.

"You think Sims will sign me when this is all over?"

"Sims will sign anything with a heartbeat that makes him cash."

"Thanks for the vote of confidence. I still have something in the tank. No bullshit."

"I know."

She gripped my hand even tighter. "Tam jerking our chain with this Sofa dude?"

"Fifty-fifty," I said.

"No bueno," she said.

I laughed. The gravel formed a straight path now, and ran alongside a road.

"I'll give you first dibs on that asshole," I said. "Lock him up with one of those triangle chokes."

"Thanks."

She let go of my hand, put both her hands on my face, turned my head toward her and kissed me for a very long time. Sans interruption. I enjoyed every bit of it, and our second kiss got way more style points than the first.

"That's platonic," she said, smiling.

"Indeed."

We sat there basking in the afterglow and would have done so for much longer if it weren't for Tam. He'd stopped his car up on the road.

He'd found us.

"I'm sorry," he said, getting out.

He walked off the roadway and down to the path.

I said nothing.

14

I feigned a jab and Tam covered his face. He stayed that way for a few seconds, and then when he realized I hadn't thrown anything, he lowered his hands.

To the victor go the spoils.

I struck him with the heel pad of my hand and Tam fell back, grabbing his jaw. I went easy on him, but not for long.

"You really wanna lose your throwing hand, asshole?"

I clenched my fists, got into a boxing stance, and crowded him. I hated to get all formal on the hombre, but his brain needed some recalibration. Teach his candy ass not to mess with amateur sleuths trying to get answers about an autistic kid who grew up around the fight game.

Tam backed up and played the only card he had left. The pity card.

"Gedrin, I'm sorry, man. I didn't mean to. The button's for emergencies. I can't be having any which person making threats in my home. I've got a wife and kids and a damned dog. And the Saints have eyes and ears everywhere. They think I'm dishing out on them and it all goes to shit."

I hardened my eyes and prepared for the kill. But then I remembered Leslie, and that gave me pause. If I discombobulated Tam, the poor fur baby would go fatherless. The effects on Leslie would be disastrous, and there was a very good chance they'd end up throwing the chap in a pound somewhere because of misbehavior, when in reality it'd be canine grief and lack of adjustment. Then some asshole would pick him up as a Christmas toy for the family, get tired of him, send him back to the shelter, and repeat the process all over again.

I thought of Henri, and the decision was clear.

For now, I'd let Tam keep his faculties intact.

"Call off your boys," I said.

Tam backed up a step. "I don't have any boys."

I punched him in the thigh. A low warning shot. He winced and grabbed it.

"At the gate," I said. "The guards. The button summons them, right?"

Tam shook his head. "No. They just man the gate. An outside security firm the community contracts with comes in."

"Call them off."

He flinched before I even did anything. For a big tough quarterback who took a lot of hits, he was a pussy.

He put his hands back up. "Okay. Done."

He made a call and waited for a few seconds.

Then he said, "Jerry, false alarm. The big doggo tripped it again. Take care."

He hung up the phone and put it in his pocket.

"See?" He put his hands up again. "I'm sorry, Gedrin."

I was ready to punch him in the liver, but Devin beat me to it. She connected with a solid shot, and Tam keeled over. Great minds think alike.

"I almost married a lawman once," she said. "Too much drama."

I helped Tam up, and he looked like he was about to cry.

"We're just having some fun," I said.

He covered his face with his hands.

"I could bash your face in in two seconds if I really wanted to, even if you cover up," I said. "Give it up."

It was solid logic, and Tam lowered his hands.

"That shit about Sofa true or are you jerking us?" Devin said. "I don't want to run in circles around this town while my brother is getting owned out there by some sick fuck."

Tam nodded. "On my mama's grave. Mario is a bad cat. He runs a whole lot of shit. My bet's he has him or knows who does."

"Fuck the histrionics," I said. "Am I shaking?"

Tam shook his head.

"Then give up the stock lines and fess the hell up. Where's Sofa at?"

"He moves around a lot. And that was back then. I don't know now, man. I haven't heard from him since all the shit hit the fan."

I clenched my fists.

"I swear, Gedrin. Would I be back here to give you more shit? Just for kicks?"

I thought about it some more. Maybe he was Sofa's foil. Sent to lull us into a false sense of security before the Saints pounced on us.

But then again, the more Tam talked the more he seemed like a stupid-ass jock who'd taken too many hits. Like moi.

"Cut it," I said. "Where was he stationed before?"

"When?"

"Whenever."

I stared Tam down. On the one hand he did seem worked up about hitting the panic button on me and Devin, and it made sense that he'd come find us to make amends from earlier.

Amends with two celebs who could put him back on the map. But on the other hand, I'd learned never to trust hombres who were once in the limelight. They were natural rabble-rousers and knew how to play both sides for maximum effect. Tam had been getting bribes from the time he hit puberty, and he was used to people kissing his ass.

Not me.

I kicked asses and took names.

Tam looked over at the road, which was completely empty. It was a backroad of some sort, not a major thoroughfare. The silence was eerie.

"When I was at UT, Mario drove me to and from campus," Tam said. "Back then, I signed with Anton, before I signed with Sims. It was a brief dalliance on the dark side. That final year before I turned pro. I don't like sharing it, but it's true. Anton set it all up. The rides back and forth. The excused absences. It got to the point where Mario even wanted to drive me to the away games, but the school nipped that in the bud. Can't have players calling all the shots, even if they're the heart of the team, you feel me?"

"Bullshit," I said. "You ignored the Saints your first three years?"

"I didn't need them. Then the acclaim really got hot my senior year and the threats started rolling in. Everybody wanted a piece of me, good or bad. I needed protection."

"And the school never caught wind that you hired an agent?"

At the time college athletes couldn't hire agents, especially with one whole year of college eligibility left.

Tam nodded. "Anton was the shadiest dude I've ever been with, but he knew how to play it. I never signed shit and all our meetings were on the road."

That jibed, so I rolled with it.

"This was years ago, Gedrin. Mario lived in a small place in Pecan Valley. No security on the outside, but hell were they packing on the inside. Mario brought me inside once to say hello to the boys, and they'd gamble about how many picks I'd throw and the usual crooked shit. Then he drove me to the games."

Tam gave us the address, and Devin put it in her phone.

"Not too far," Devin said.

Tam looked concerned. "The Saints move around a lot. They're not that stupid to live in the same flophouse forever. Watch your back, Gedrin. These dudes don't play by the rules. And Devin, I hope you find your bro. I really do. But there's some doors you just don't go knocking on. If there's another way, go for it. Things are meaner out here in Texas."

He put his head in his hands. "And now, I'm fucked. The Saints don't do well with snitches. Remember that when you're running all over town."

"We're not narcs," Devin said.

"Don't matter to these people."

He was right. The underworld never gave a shit about appearances. It was a dog-eat-dog world. To get respect you had to gain respect. And when that trust went out the window, all those in the orbit had an immediate expiration date. I'd done time with the same peeps over and over.

Tam was right. He was fucked.

But so were we.

Our sleuthing was definitely on somebody's radar.

The only way out was to find Jake and take the Saints down too. I fixed the collar on Tam's shirt, and he thanked me.

"Can I have a picture?" he said. "With both of you. I forgot to ask back at the house."

I considered it for a second, but I didn't want to attract more attention from the crazy hombres out there.

"No. Get back to camp and develop a fucking superstar quarterback that you can ship to Chicago, will ya? We haven't had a star since Sid Luckman."

Oh, the Bears.

Tam shook my hand and left. His car burned rubber so fast the tires brought up plumes of smoke from the pavement.

We walked up to the road, and Devin picked something up from the asphalt. A metal pole. It looked like it'd fallen off of Tam's car. He'd driven a beater to get to us, when he had an armada of luxury on the ridge.

"You collecting metals, missy?"

Devin smiled. "I never shy away from a street fight."

"My kind of girl."

We walked to the nearest main road, found a cab, and took it to Pecan Valley.

15

Sofa's place needed some serious landscaping. The grass was seven inches tall with an atrocious brown hue, the driveway was crooked in all the corners, and the front stoop was so cracked the city ordinance peeps would have a field day.

I looked around for a hose or a sprinkler and came up empty. Lack of hydration affected brain bashers and grass too. No bueno. The sun's rays didn't play. If I had to make an educated guess, the last time anybody had given a shit about the lot was when Tam had two good knees.

I scanned the driveway for any signs of life. It was empty, and the garage was in need of a paint job. I could see the yard through the chain-link fence, but I couldn't see any movement. Tam had warned us to be prepared for armed foes, but the only fight worth having at this point was whether or not to hop the fence or just take my chances and ring the bell.

I wanted the option that carried with it the highest probability of conflict. I was itching for a fight after Devin had done her handiwork on the riverwalk. That, and it didn't hurt to impress.

I walked up to the front stoop and rang the bell. Devin stood a few feet back, keeping a lookout for nosy neighbors and a potential ambush. She scanned the perimeter and shook her head, giving the all-clear.

I waited several seconds.

Nada.

I tried to peer through the small windowpane at the top of the door, but I couldn't make anything out. I rang the bell a second time, and still nobody answered. My foot strength wasn't all that hot so I couldn't kick the door down. I knocked.

Nada.

I looked back at Devin, and she held her hands up. Two sleuths running into typical sleuth problems.

I shook the door handle, and at first it didn't budge, but then it opened right up. I put my hands up expecting to throw down on anything that moved, but to my surprise all was still inside. The door creaked badly as it opened into a living room that would make the best of hoarders proud. Yellow newspapers lined every inch of the living space, with cardboard boxes hanging off of a three-piece brown sectional couch with a whole bunch of stains on it. Several hampers of clothes were tossed upside down in one corner, and some stray condom wrappers were stuck to the dirty carpet in the middle of the room.

"I smell groupie," Devin said.

"Oy vey," I said.

Devin shook her head and we made our way into the kitchen, where we found the motherlode.

Biker jackets of all sizes were piled up on the table. A stack of shoulder patches lay next to the jackets, and pieces of thread peeked out of some of the jacket sleeves, like a seamstress had run out of time. I picked up one of the patches and analyzed the handiwork. On a scale of one to ten, I rated it a solid six point five. The yellow emblem was off line a few inches from the edge of the fabric, and I couldn't quite make out the S in "Saints."

Sofa's home was a ranch-style, which meant that the bedrooms, kitchen, and bathroom all sat on the main level, with the basement down below. I'd learned all that from Sims, who was always trying to get me to settle down and become a property owner. I of course preferred my nomad motel status, but I did enjoy learning new vocabulary from time to time. This ranch had two bedrooms, and Devin wanted to hurry up and search them, but I wanted weaponry first, in case Tam was right. I looked through the kitchen cabinets, under the kitchen table, and around all the appliances. I came up empty. Then I went back into the living room and looked around the hoarder goodness. It took me several seconds, but I found what I needed.

A fireplace poker. Two of them in fact. All rusted out, but still easy to use to bludgeon bad hombres with.

"Go easy on the handle," I said to Devin, handing her a poker.

"That's no fun."

She made wide, circular cuts in the air and smiled. Then she told me about her presser again. It was in a few hours, but given the way things were going I had a hard time envisioning a scenario where we found Jake and made it to the presser in time to field questions from all the sharks. It was just past four in the afternoon. But optimism is muy bueno in the amateur sleuth game, so I rolled with it.

I walked to the first bedroom and kicked the door in. It was unlocked so my motion looked like a pro's. This room was even more depressing than the living room. There was nothing here but a fuzzy green carpet that curled up in all the corners of the room, along with a box of nails lying in the middle of the floor.

Devin walked ahead of me to the second bedroom. I motioned her to step back so I could kick it down, but she shook her head and just turned the knob.

She opened the door slowly, and I stepped through the void.

I was attacked instantly.

Not by Sofa or any of the Saints.

But by a Siberian husky.

He bowled me over like a bag of Swiss cheese and started sniffing my armpits. Devin laughed, and the husky increased his zeal. I'd learned long ago with Henri that the key to gaining a dog's trust upon initial meet-and-greet is to stand still like a statue. Let the canine investigate and live to fight another day.

I closed my eyes, and the husky knocked me to the ground again. He investigated my whole body. Or at least half of it. He went from my pits to my stomach to my kneecaps. Then he pulled away and started whining. I tried to soothe the chap, but he just got louder and louder.

"Poor thing probably hasn't had anything to eat," Devin said.

She looked around for some food, but the room was empty, apart from some dog toys.

The husky ran down the hall and started pawing at the door to the basement. Whining. Pawing. Whining. Pawing.

I opened the door, and the husky's whines got even louder. He peered down the steps into the darkness, but hung back.

I flipped the switch at the top of the steps. Nothing happened.

"You have any light on that fruit phone?" I said.

"What are you smoking?" Devin said.

"The fruit. The back." I pointed to the camera on the back of her phone, and Devin smiled.

She activated the camera with a touch of a button and shined it on the light switch. I tried again, but still nothing doing.

"The cavalry is waiting," I said. "Keep her steady."

Devin clenched her fire poker and phone. "Bring it on."

I walked slowly down the steps while Devin shone her light from above. She tried to get the husky to come down with us, but he appeared scarred for life and didn't move from his perch.

When I got to the bottom, there was no cavalry in sight. That damned Tam. The water heater was singing and an old TV was playing static in a corner. A recliner that had seen better days sat in front it, and I half expected somebody to jump out and own our candy asses, but the chair was empty.

Devin kept shining the light as we walked around the basement. The Saints had more jackets down here, along with various documents. I saw a seamstress table and a corkboard too. At one point the hombres must have had meetings down here. But before I could read any of their marketing materials, I heard a crash out front. I gripped the poker hard and crouched below one of the high windows, peering into the front yard.

The mailman had scraped the curb with his truck.

I turned away, intending to search every nook and cranny of the place.

That was when I tripped over a body.

16

A very large man lay facedown in a pool of his own blood. The husky wailed from the top of the steps, and it all made sense. A canine wails for its beloved departed owner.

Devin held her nose and handed me the phone.

While the average hombre was intimidated by death and all its iterations, I marched to a different drum. I'd seen it all inside and outside the ring. From grown men losing control of their faculties between the ropes to gangbangers severing carotid arteries on the yard to counselors blowing their brains out in fancy high-rises.

Death was all part of the game. There was no escaping it, though perhaps the circumstances could be scripted better in some cases.

I knelt down and shone the light on the man's body. He was wearing a biker jacket with holes by his tailbone area. I shone the light closer. The holes seemed to match a very large pair of incisors. Maybe the husky wasn't so aggrieved after all and had gone for the man's ass in a hangry stupor.

I then moved the light over to the man's pockets. They were hanging inside out as if someone had riffled through them. Of course they were empty.

I then shone the light on the back of the man's head, revealing a long mane of hair that just passed the man's lower earlobes.

"Turn Fonzie over," Devin said.

I laughed, and as I took a step back I realized the man's locks definitely resembled the character she was talking about. I looked at Devin and she stuck her tongue out. I had expected her to be badass, but this amount of badass was a pleasant surprise. She was calm and collected and immune to the destruction. But then again when you're part of the fight club, everybody's wires are like that.

"Evidence," I said. "Keep it to a minimum. Especially with these khaki cowboys."

"Yes, counselor."

She stood still.

I had no desire to involve myself with the Texas criminal justice system anytime soon. My travels of late seemed to always land me in harm's way, but things were subject to change. Power of will. A pre-New Year's resolution of sorts.

Stay the fuck out of smelly cells.

I put the light on the back of the man's jacket and analyzed the writing on it. It matched the insignia from the patches in the kitchen. The "S" was once again hard to make out. But the patches in the kitchen were yellow, and this one was a mustard green. Maybe that's how the higher-ups rolled. Sofa had met his match downstairs in a shitty basement in a shitty place on an August summer day. Doesn't always pay to be a higher-up.

Or maybe this was one of Sofa's minions who had paid the price for some transgression.

I flashed the light around the man's body a couple more

times, looking for anything else important, but there was nothing.

"Sofa's too stupid for his own good," I said.

"Not him," Devin said. "He'd know the ins and outs and be prepared for war against anyone trying to harm him. Especially in his own damned place. Nobody's that stupid."

"Secret passages and shit," I said.

Devin nodded. "Unless it was from within."

I nodded. "Keep your friends close and your enemies closer."

Devin took her phone back and flashed it around the basement. There weren't any more traces of blood anywhere. Professional hit and professional cleanup.

"You think Tam jerked us?" Devin said.

"He's jerked everybody his whole life. But this one's legit." The more I thought about it, the more I realized that Tam really had nothing to gain by sending us on a wild goose chase. Hell, the hombre just wanted a damned autograph.

"Athletes are hit or miss," Devin said.

"In terms of temperament?" I said.

"The whole works."

"Agreed."

Devin smiled and we walked back upstairs. The husky licked both of us for several seconds, then got on his back for belly rubs. He'd stopped wailing but wanted plenty of cuddles. I obliged while wondering what the plan was for the chap. Turn him in to the shelter? Leave him in the house and call somebody? Or option C...

Bring him on the sleuth.

I ran the scenarios through my head, but it was really a no-brainer.

I found a leash right beside the front door on a makeshift coat rack that peeked out from the closet in the entryway. The leash was about the only thing in this place that didn't look dated. I clipped it on the husky's collar and he started doing quick circles.

"He's all yours," Devin said.

As I closed the closet door, I noticed a matchbook sitting on the top rack and pocketed it. The fire could come in handy, and there was an address on the back of it.

An amateur sleuth has to explore all avenues.

I opened the front door, and that's when everything changed.

Devin got a text on her phone.

Or to be more exact, she got a video.

"What the fuck?" she said.

She clicked on the video, and we saw Jake again. Out of the chair now, but barely able to stand. A foot came flying in from off screen, kicking him in the stomach, and Jake fell to his knees spitting up blood.

Then a voice, still off camera.

"Brainy boy, you gonna sing some more? Huh?"

The camera was shaky, but then it steadied itself, like it was placed on a tripod or a sturdy table. A buff man walked into frame. I could see his short-cropped hair, but his face was blurred. I couldn't tell if it was some special effect on the video, or if the man's face legit looked fucked up like that.

The man punched Jake in the face, and Jake went out cold for a second before curling up in a fetal position.

The buff man then turned toward the camera.

"I see you found one of our hideouts. And one of our former brothers. When you don't follow the way, that's what happens. Good thing both of you are in the public eye. What do we call you? Celebs, famous people, or athletes? Eh, let's go with rich assholes. Good thing you're watching this, then. Bring ten million cash and this all ends tonight. I know you're good for it. Wait for the spot."

The man laughed, then walked over to Jake. He looked at Jake, then back at the camera, then back at Jake again.

He pulled a knife out of his pocket and sliced Jake's forearm. As he went for another slice, the video went black.

17

"If they finish Jake, they might as well finish me," Devin said. She was back at my motel, wiping her wet lashes. I'd taken her and the husky back to my place to regroup. The video had pushed Devin over the edge, and her calm demeanor from earlier had morphed into a cold, frightened rage.

"One more move like that and I'm gonna decapitate him," she said.

"Good."

I hugged Devin, and she sank into my arms for a very long time. When we were done, I got a water bottle from my fridge and she went to the bathroom. The husky lay down at the foot of the bed, yawned, looked away, and started napping. I still didn't know what role he would play in the investigation, but I figured he'd be better off with a canine lover than with a volunteer who only took him out of his cage here and there while waiting for prospective adopters to take to him.

I heard Devin rustling the cabinets in the bathroom and

sniffling, but I let it be. Sometimes it's better to let things resolve themselves in due course.

The videographer had struck a nerve, but it was only a matter of time before I got ahold of him by the throat and showed him what happened to those who disrespected family in the fight game. I'd promised Devin I'd give her the first shot, but as I sat on my bed I wondered in the moment whether I'd be able to hold up my end of the bargain. When things got ugly, I couldn't hold back sometimes. Like a pack of hyenas that launched into their prey when they got it down, I couldn't relent. This notemaker-videographer hombre was gonna get his face twisted no matter what.

I smiled and pictured the Picasso I'd make with his face. I didn't tell Devin any of these finer details. Some things are better left unsaid.

Real violent things.

Before we could get there though, there was the matter of cash. Devin didn't have it and told me as much on the way to my place. I was confident that I could swing it, but there were many different ways to do so. If the videographer had struck before I'd gone to Pontiac, I could have withdrawn the money on the spot. Sims would have pulled some strings and I'd have the bills neatly wrapped in suitcases. Now, I had to be more creative. Lawyer fees had eaten much of my net worth over the years, and sponsors had avoided me like the plague after I got out. But things were looking up, and Sims had gotten me some new endorsers who were confident as hell about my innocence. And then there were the fight contracts I had on the horizon. If I got my belt back.

Long story short, I could swing ten mill. But I didn't want to. Leverage was a beautiful thing, and any criminal worth his or her salt understood the basic principle. The minute I came up with the cash, the videographer hombre would proceed to his next request. Up the ante. Monkey see, monkey do.

He'd ask for more and more and more.

And I'd pay to play.

Poor Jake.

The kid was toughing it out, and they'd keep him alive because they knew he was their meal ticket. But the psychological toll on an already fragile brain would be endless. Devin might get her brother back, but he wouldn't be the same. I didn't know the nuances of autism, but I figured that a multitude of stressful events would make for a multitude of autism problems.

My mind went back to the video. The buff man hadn't been wearing a Saints jacket, and he had short-cropped hair. Maybe he was the man for hire in kidnapping scenarios, or maybe he'd forgotten his jacket at home. His voice had been muffled, and I now wondered if he was using some kind of emulator to mask his true voice. People could do a whole bunch of shit nowadays with those fruit phones.

Bottom line, the gang had paid the price because Jake had snitched. He wasn't the first and he certainly wouldn't be the last, but the gang never forgives and never forgets. They'd remind him of that.

If Jake made it out of this at all.

I was pondering different scenarios in my head when Devin came out of the bathroom.

"Sorry," she said. "It's been a fucking day."

She sat on the edge of the bed and buried her head in my chest. I held her there again, and she sniffled and buried her head deeper.

"This kid's been through so much," she said. "I'm the worst sister."

I rubbed her shoulders. "As long as they think we're playing ball, he's not going anywhere."

She nodded and wiped some of her sniffles away.

The husky must have picked up on our cues, because he woke up, padded over, and started licking Devin's hands.

She laughed.

"I'm ticklish and he knows it."

The husky wagged his tail and tackled her on the bed. Devin ate up every second of it. She was a natural. Then the husky jumped off the bed, spent, and sauntered off toward the kitchen area.

"That was something," she said.

"I'll say."

I told her the plan. In detail. I left no stone unturned. She nodded her head at times and shook her head at others. She even modified the plan some, but by and large we were in agreement.

We knew the play, and it was just matter of execution.

I got up from the bed and went to the mini-fridge. I always preferred rooms with beverage storage. I got myself a glass of OJ and filled up a glass of water for Devin. I needed some sugar and figured it would give me some extra oomph to keep on sleuthing.

I gave the husky some water too, then handed Devin her glass.

"More vitamin C, more knockout power," I said. "Sleuth basics."

"I appreciate the wisdom," she said. "But I thought champs were born ready?"

She gave me a mischievous look, and I returned it. While my track record with the female sex was quite low in the grand scheme of things, my track record when the time came to get physical was flawless.

Maybe it was because many women fantasized about hitting the sheets with someone they've seen on TV, or maybe it was because they implicitly knew that I wouldn't kiss and tell. The Gedrin experience was really something. Or maybe it was none of the above.

That's how I rolled.

Devin took the glass of OJ out of my hands and put it on the nightstand.

"Why thank you," I said.

She put her glass on the nightstand, pushed me down on the bed, and ran her hands down my chest super slow. She said nothing. Then she made her way to my abs and did small circles with her index fingers. She avoided my flank, which was good because that was my ticklish spot.

Then she made her way further down and stayed there.

18

I didn't object. Devin made even bigger circles with her hands on my thighs. She ran them clockwise for a few seconds, then counterclockwise. I smiled and was about to say something stupid, but she shushed me and climbed on top of me.

I closed my eyes. I learned long ago that following orders was muy bueno in the bedroom and it made for a more sensual experience.

Devin ordered me to take my shirt off, and I obliged. She undid my belt.

"You're all mine, champ."

"Excellente," I said.

She pulled my pants down and wiggled me out of them. She tossed those too, and that left my boxers.

"Wow," she said.

"Say it again."

She smiled, and I returned it. My boxers were black, with large white lettering across the front that said "I Love Maple Syrup." Sims knew about the infamous t-shirt bearing the same words that I'd worn at a presser once, but he had no idea I'd swung a separate deal for the boxers and would do a photo shoot soon. Shysters needed to be kept in the dark sometimes.

"Organic," I said.

Devin shook her head, took off my boxers and tossed those farther than the rest.

"What are you gonna do to me?" she said.

Her voice was sexy and playful, and I gave a sexy, playful response.

And then we ran out of things to say.

Devin did things with her mouth that had me spasming in pleasure for an eternity. A wise man once said there's a first time for everything, and damn, ain't that the truth. I'd prided myself on calling the shots in the bedroom and lasting like a stallion.

But she had other plans.

She kept doing things with her mouth and I kept spasming. The tension was real and then the train left the station. I came so hard that I tore the sheets where my palms were.

"Damn, champ. You've been deprived."

She smiled and lay down on the pillow next to me. We cuddled, held hands, and massaged each other. I was basking in the afterglow, but I was just getting started. I might not have lasted like a stallion in round one, but I sure as hell would in round two.

Champs recover instantly.

I worked my hands down Devin's thighs, and then it was my turn to use my mouth.

I had no objection.

Devin squirmed and said my name so many times it almost went out of style. She clutched the headboard so tight I thought she'd rip it off the wall. Eventually her train left the station too and she came. The sheets on her side of the bed were intact, but her hair was a spectacle.

We basked in the afterglow for several seconds.

But she wasn't done, and neither was I. She was a champ, and I was a champ. Our drives were insatiable.

I pulled her close and we fucked. Again and again and again and again. When we finally collapsed on the sheets our bodies were like some of the strangest pretzels I'd ever seen.

"Gedrin, Gedrin..."

She said my name real soothingly this time.

"Get used to it," I said. "There's more what that came from."

She punched me and we cuddled. Oxytocin really is a beautiful thing. I'm not sure how long we lay there in each other's arms, but apparently it was too long.

I got a text on my phone. Doggy daycare was closing soon.

We got ready in record time and left the motel.

Henri was about to make a new friend.

19

We were one minute late and the girl at the front desk acted like it was the biggest sin of all time.

"We close at six," the girl said.

"There was extraterrestrial activity out there," I said.

The girl rolled her eyes and went back to get Henri. The play area was a deserted wasteland now. Bowls and leashes and toys lay scattered about at all angles. Pet deodorizer wafted from the floors, and I wondered if Henri was the culprit, or one of his enemies.

I'd told Devin and the husky to wait outside. Introductions were not Henri's strong suit, though he'd made a great amount of progress since I'd entered his life. I figured I would soothe Henri when he came out looking all fresh from his play and groom session, and then I'd make the connection.

The husky didn't seem to have a name, so I'd come up with a short one-syllable version on the spot and let canine pals be canine pals.

The girl came out a minute later and Henri gave me the silent treatment. His fur was neatly combed and he smelled like a bunch of lilacs. He looked ten pounds lighter too from the FURminator brushing. I gave Henri the silent treatment back, and the girl gave both of us a quizzical look.

Then I got down on all fours like a canine. Henri looked away. He twisted his left ear one way and his right ear the other. Confusion was the name of the game.

"Sir, we need to close up."

I ignored the girl because I was too focused on the task at hand.

Getting back in Henri's good graces.

Henri slowly turned his head toward me, wary.

I inched closer and went for it.

"Henri, you want some food?"

He caved and jumped into my arms, tail wagging all over the place. He licked me up and down and squealed like a puppy. The girl at the desk must have been moved, because she didn't say another word about closing. I took a duck biscuit out of my pocket and Henri gulped it down in record time. I'd picked up a bag on the way over and figured the husky would approve too.

"Gracias," I said, walking out.

The girl locked up behind me.

And that's when Henri came face to face with the husky. The smell-off lasted for an eternity, but Henri didn't show even a hint of teeth.

"Henri, meet Husker," I said. "Husker, meet Henri."

"How original," Devin said.

Husker did several circles, but it was hard to rein him in.

"Where's his collar?" I said.

"It fell off when you were inside. Criminals invest in cheap things."

I shook my head and knocked on the door. The girl opened back up and I explained the situation. After much back and forth she finally gave me a collar, and I gave her a donation.

"You're trouble," Devin said.

"Preach," I said.

I put the collar on Husker and reattached the leash. Henri started play-growling. This was a great sign, so I loosened my leash and Devin did the same on her end. The canines frolicked and got down on all fours and pretended to chase each other a little bit. Then they wagged their tails like bosses and fell in line at their handlers' hips.

"Let's roll," I said.

"You really are a dog whisperer," Devin said.

"I have many talents."

"I'll say."

She grinned, and we kept moving. Now the focus returned to sleuthing. The notetaker-videographer wanted cash, and I would give it and then some.

On my terms.

I told Devin the place, and she told me we could walk there. So we did. I don't remember how long it took, but I do remember that Henri and Husker got several compliments on the walk over from passersby.

When we finally arrived at our destination, I handed Devin Henri's leash.

"Wait here," I said.

We were at a fixer-upper apartment building on the outskirts of San Antonio. Or thereabouts. I was becoming an expert at looking at maps on the Jitterbug. Old Faithful didn't disappoint. It was truly a gem for its price tag.

Devin seemed annoyed for a second, then she let it be. I walked up two flights of stairs, knocked on the third door at the end of the hall and was let in by a very large Filipino man in a San Antonio Spurs flat cap.

When I got inside, I looked around at the multiple sets of eyes gazing back at me. I stared at them all, one by one, never blinking, but scanning and surveying for my quarry.

When I found him, I said absolutely nada.

That was part of the plan.

My quarry was a skinny black man who hadn't hit the gym in ages. But looks were deceiving. He was a black belt in jiujitsu, and I'd learned the hard way once that he could twist hombres like a serpent and send them to urgent care.

"Gedrin. Long time you piece of shit."

He smiled, and I returned it.

"The law works in mysterious ways, Felix."

We bro-hugged, and the men around him relaxed instantaneously.

"You roll with a dog pack, bro? My boys were spying from up here."

"The best defense is a pair of big-ass canines."

Felix grinned. "Or just throw hands and no need for defense, right?"

I grinned too.

Felix walked into another room and returned with a duffel bag. "Gedrin, I know you're good for it, so take your time with it. You sure you don't need any muscle?"

Felix flexed his biceps, and I saw a sliver of definition, but that wasn't saying much. Where we were headed, we needed people to throw down, not get thrown down and put into pretzels.

"You got ground game," I said, "but I don't need that shit."

He nodded. "Murdock done told me that. How's cuz doing anyways?"

"Last I saw him he was eating a Portillos Italian Beef with the sauce on the side."

"The motherfucker still wants it on the side. I'ma visit his ass in Chicago one day, but I don't like them polar vortexes and shit."

"They're getting worse," I said. "Stick it out here with the khaki boys."

Felix laughed, and we bro-hugged. And just like that I was out. I walked back down the stairs and out to the street.

But everybody was gone.

I walked around the corner, and still nada.

Then I walked back to the front. Devin had reappeared with our furry companions.

"They had to potty and were picky about their spots," she said. "Somebody was feeding them too many biscuits."

I smiled and held up the duffel bag. "Time to kick some ass."

"I thought you'd never ask."

We walked south, and that's when Devin got another text. She held it up for me to see. This one was tamer than before. No video. Just a short message.

Don't be late, cutie.

Followed by an address.

I clutched the duffel bag a little tighter and smiled. We were one step closer to freeing Jake.

20

The address led us to an old warehouse on the outer edge of the city. The only way in was through a dilapidated metal fence that had been cut at the corners and pulled back way too many times. 'Twas a trespasser's paradise.

I pulled back the fence and Devin went through with the canines. They were enjoying the excursion mucho, and they let out some playful barks. I shushed them as I pushed through the fence.

All was quiet.

I could make out some lights through one of the grimy windows on the upper floor of the warehouse, but I couldn't make out any activity. The light seemed to come and go, and after I stared at it for a few seconds, it finally fizzled out altogether.

"Showtime," Devin said.

"Not so fast," I said.

As much as I wanted to run up the stairs, bust the door down, and start going to town on various heels, I had to play the odds. Two champs versus a potentially infinite number of armed hombres. The fireplace pokers could prick an arm or two, but they were more novelty than substance.

I scanned the warehouse again for any movement and came up empty. There were two floors and two wide double doors at the top of a winding pair of steps. The same kind that often doubled as fire escapes in the Big Apple. I wondered if the second floor was the distraction for the first-floor cavalry to come.

I gripped my poker hard and started walking slowly toward the stairs. The more I walked the more I saw remnants of an old metal factory. Stray bits lined the underside of the stairs and rusty chunks ran parallel to the fence line. I pointed it all out to Devin so she could maneuver the canines appropriately.

It took us twelve seconds to reach the bottom of the steps.

But we never made it up because a few seconds after that we were surrounded.

By the hombres from the riverwalk. And some new hombres I couldn't quite place. They came from the fences and they formed a very large semicircle around us.

Henri barked, and so did Husker, but the hombres were undeterred. They pressed closer, and there was no way out. I counted ten easy. But really it was eleven because somebody rolled up in a Jeep Wrangler and pointed his high beams right at me.

I squinted through the light, but it only made things worse. The light pierced my pupils and I saw small halos out of the corners. Too damned bright. Then a voice sounded over the rumble of the Jeep's engine.

"Two champs putting their nose where it doesn't fucking belong."

I couldn't tell where the voice was coming from. It sounded

like it was to the left of the Jeep, then to the right of the Jeep, then behind the Jeep.

The voice grew louder.

"When you ask for a fair wage for a day's work, you expect to get it and then some. You have that stash, champ?"

I tried opening my eyes more, but still nothing doing.

"Come closer and we'll have a party," I said.

The voice laughed, and it was one of those hyena laughs that you see in animated films.

All was silent for a beat, then the high beams flicked down, leaving just the headlights. Still bright, but not blinding.

My eyes adjusted and I got the picture.

Eight more hombres, plus one additional hombre behind the wheel of the Jeep. He hopped off, and the rest of the dudes inched ever closer.

The driver came forward. He didn't seem buff, so he didn't make the cut as the videographer, but every other guy in the circle qualified for the role. They looked like they did three-a-days.

"Drop the bag," he said.

"Say it to my face," I said.

"Pride. I like that," the man said.

He wore a tight-fitting teal t-shirt and khaki pants with some construction boots. He was tatted up on his right arm, but his left was clean.

He came within a few feet of me.

"Hand the bag over or I'm taking those fucking dogs too."

I looked at Henri and Henri looked at me and Husker looked at Devin and Devin looked at me and smiled.

She knew what was about to go down.

I nodded my head, took Henri's leash, and gave it to Devin. The buildup to a fight was always great. Your body was fighting the euphoria of a potential victory and your heart was ramping up to the reality that it could beat its very last breath if the right shots hit at the right times. The signals ran a million miles an hour and never went out of style.

I rolled up my sleeves, even though there wasn't much space to roll them up since I always wore slim t-shirts anyway. Mine were crisper than the teal man's though, even though I often put them through the wringer.

With assholes like this.

I did a few neck circles, then I turned my attention back to the teal man.

"Touch one hair on my dog's head and you'll be sucking shakes out of a fucking tube the rest of your life."

The teal man laughed again, less hyena-like this time, but still annoying as hell.

"A prideful jokester. Even better. Challenge accepted."

He pounced.

In the ring I always used the first round to feel my opponent out. I wanted the knockout, but I wanted to figure out his style before getting the knockout. My fights seldom lasted long after that. Such a strategy by and large prevented me from being caught by a lucky shot and embarrassing myself all over pay-per-view.

The street was a whole other animal.

It was always best to make the first move.

But I was slow this time. The miles add up sometimes. The teal man got me with a jab, then he followed up with a hook to the body. I dropped the duffel bag and got in my fighting stance, but I knew I had my work cut out for me.

He was a southpaw.

Southpaws infuriated the hell out of me. They always seemed able to switch back and forth from orthodox to southpaw to orthodox, with a bevy of different styles too. The teal man fit the bill. He alternated between boxing stances and

Muay Thai stances and MMA stances. He threw jabs and hooks and uppercuts that mostly hit air, but some of them connected.

Unfortunately, accumulation of damage is a thing in video games and in real life. The more hits one takes, the closer one gets to extinction. And I'd taken a hell of a lot of hits in my time, both in the ring and out. Anybody with half an eye could see that my recovery just wasn't what it used to be.

I held my side for a minute and gritted my teeth.

"Winded, champ?" The teal man smiled and got me with another jab.

I shook it off, faked a jab, then got him with a jab. One of my favorite tricks. The teal man woke up. He put his guard up a little higher and closed his stance a little.

"Jake bit off more than he could chew," he said.

He tried to kick me, but I checked it. I'd taken some Muay Thai classes one summer, much to Sal's dismay. He hated when I mixed styles and got distracted from my craft.

But all's fair on the streets, boyo.

I faked a kick of my own and got the teal man with a right elbow to the face. He fell to the ground as a cut opened up on his forehead.

And then all hell broke loose.

All the hombres in the circle charged me, throwing elbows and haymakers and kicks. They were clearly neophytes though, because very few shots connected and those that did didn't have much oomph to them. I fought them off one by one. Slipping, throwing feints, ducking, delivering. Defense is the best offense sometimes.

I don't remember how many hombres I knocked out, but it was a good number. I heard Henri barking in the background, and that egged me on. For his sake as well as my own. Self-preservation is a beautiful thing.

The teal man kicked me in the back, but it was more of a graze with his shoe. I turned around and got him with an uppercut to the right kidney. He keeled back.

"Leave family alone, asshole."

I got him good with a left hook to the left kidney, and he was down again for the count.

But pride cometh before the fall. In every fight, whether sanctioned or not, there is one moment that turns the tide. All it takes is a millisecond and things are never the same again.

One of the hombres connected with a baseball bat to my left ass cheek. Pins and needles shot through my body and I couldn't stand for several seconds. Stingers were no bueno.

Then, just as I was making my way back up, the teal man kicked me square in the face. I saw two teal men, then three, then four, then one again.

"Fucker, I own you," he said.

He backed up a few steps, and I knew where this was headed. The running finisher kick.

The knockout shot.

The highlight reel.

I pushed my body up, but the pins and needles got stronger. I closed my eyes, clenched my teeth, and pushed.

But nada.

The teal man started running. As he got closer, he swung his right leg back and brought it forward. I saw his heel, then his toe. Then I saw Devin get him with a roundhouse kick square to the jaw.

The teal man collapsed like a bag of sand.

A true knockout.

The hombre with the bat came flying in for another shot, but Devin got him with a clean body shot and then choked him out in seconds.

My body decided to start working again, and I pushed

myself up. An hombre came from my blind side, and I elbowed him into next week.

And just like that, there were four left standing.

Me, Devin, Henri, and Husker.

I shook the cobwebs off, and Devin smiled.

"Champ, you look so sexy when you're down."

"Down, but never out."

We kissed, but the moment was fleeting.

Devin got another text on her phone.

"You think you can fuck with the Saints? I said ten mill, now it's twenty. Call the cops and Jakey's getting another piece taken out of him. You think we're playing? Here's the first."

The text was followed by a picture of a severed thumb, blood pooling from the detachment site.

I looked back at where I'd left the duffel bag. It was gone. There were some stray bills left in its place. Showcasing the fake bills Felix had put in there.

No bueno.

21

I made another call. This time to a connect with real cash. No bullshit. The Felix route had been intended to call the Saints' bluff, and they'd blown it out of the water. My new connect texted me a new location, and away we went.

After the thumb, Devin went silent on me. She didn't hold my hand and she didn't give me seductive gazes. I expected as much. Love was a fickle beast, and a thumb was a very important appendage in the grand scheme of things. Jake's scooping skills were in jeopardy.

I blamed Husker for the silent treatment too. He was pulling throughout the walk and not even Henri's nudges could tame the beast. And he was strong. He should have been sixty pounds—that would have been a healthy weight for the breed—but the Saints must have been feeding him too many sweets, because Husker was eighty pounds for sure. How any member of the Saints managed to rein him in was beyond me. I was impressed by his temperament though, considering his prior handlers. Aside from the play-growling session earlier, he seemed harmless.

We picked up speed with the dogs and crossed a few busy intersections with tourists taking in the carnitas scene. I was hungry again, but a mission is a mission. No way in hell I was quitting on Jake now.

We walked a few more blocks and the restaurants started fading into mid-size lawns and cozy condo buildings. I double-checked the address on my phone, and a couple minutes later we found our destination.

A mid-rise condo building painted brown with red railings overlooking a small courtyard.

"I'm coming up," Devin said.

"Glad to not be on the shit list again."

"Sorry. You know how it goes."

"I most certainly do."

Devin rubbed my shoulders in a non-seductive way. She was resolute, with that fire back in her eyes. I walked to the front gate and was about to dial the right number when Devin's phone rang.

She must have thought it was another threat from the note-taker hombre because she put it on speaker. But instead it was a fight promoter. I could spot them a million miles away. Straight, to the point. Logistics. No pleasantries.

"There's been a security threat at the arena tonight," the promoter said. "The presser is still taking place. Via Zoom. Details to follow in the next hour. Make sure you have a stable internet connection and don't be late."

The line went dead.

"You negotiate high-speed into your contract?" I said.

"Fuck them," Devin said. "Complimentary Wi-Fi or bust. If they wanna sue me, sue me."

"Spoken like a true shyster."

I dialed the number. A voice I didn't recognize came over

the intercom and asked what my business was. After I gave just the right amount of information, we were buzzed up.

"You have some interesting friends," Devin said.

"When you make people rich you can play that card all fucking day."

She nodded, then looked me up and down. More pensive this time.

"All my life I wanted a little bit of action on the outside," she said. "Not sanctioned warfare in a cage. Something movie-like that I'll never forget when I kick the bucket. I'm glad I'm in the thick of it and you're by my side. Thanks, Gedrin."

"De nada," I said. "You make an excellent sparring companion."

We walked through the courtyard to the elevators. We took one to the fourth floor and found the unit tucked away at the south end of the floor, right off a set of stairs that led back down to a different portion of the courtyard.

I knocked on the door, and my connect came out with a duffel bag. He didn't exchange any pleasantries, and I didn't expect any. He was the real deal. If Felix was the mom-and-pop operation, this hombre was Jerry Maguire. Crisp. Calm. Collected.

"Tell Sims I'm still waiting on my floor seats at the Garden."

"Get in line, I've got dibs."

"Fuck you, Gedrin."

"That's what she said. Again."

Devin laughed and the hombre shut the door in my face. Sims owed him much more than floor seats, but that was a matter between shysters.

We took the back stairs down to the courtyard, let the dogs potty, and then found the front gate again.

"He was a pleasure," Devin said.

"Indeed."

I unzipped the bag and she took a peek. It was all there.

"You're really something," she said. "You always play the scenarios like that in your head? Impressive for someone with brain damage."

"I haven't graduated to the upper echelons of sleuthdom, but that's the goal, missy. You get to the top and everybody wants a piece. But quid pro quo is the best game in town."

Devin nodded.

"Should we count it?" she said.

"Please."

I zipped the bag up and we walked away from the building. Devin got another text five minutes later. From the notemaker this time. No pictures or videos. Just coordinates.

She shook her head and handed me Husker's leash. She furrowed her brows and racked her brain for something to text back.

I took the phone from her and made it real simple.

Proof of life, I texted.

I waited for the three dots to pop up telling me that the recipient not only had a fruit phone but was texting back.

Nada.

Devin gritted her teeth.

Then the dots popped up.

And disappeared.

Popped up.

And disappeared.

Mind games.

We stopped at a random street corner in San Antonio for who knows how long. Flimsy brain cells are the real deal.

Then the dots came back.

And a video appeared.
Jakey sitting on the chair, cut up and fucked up.
But alive.
I didn't notice any missing thumbs.

22

Devin honored her contract. Thirty minutes after getting proof of life she was parked in front of her computer in her hotel room setting up for the Zoom presser. She'd requested a folding table from the concierge downstairs, and a twenty-foot monstrosity had been brought up in record time and parked right in the middle of the living space. To the right of her computer she had a legal pad, and to the left a cup of joe.

"You asking the sharks questions?" I said.

"I'm gonna draw some crustaceans," she said. "I can turn my video off and work on my craft."

She explained all the ins and outs of the Zoom platform. Sims had mentioned something to me about using it for the next fight, but I didn't understand it and I didn't want it. I'd forgotten the conversation faster than you can say conversation. Face to face—that's how pressers were meant to be. If it couldn't be done, then there wouldn't be one at all.

I gathered from Devin's explanation that the platform essentially was a slightly more dressed-up version of video on the fruit phones. Chats and rooms and call-ins and more. No bueno.

As Devin got in position to start, I sat off-camera on the other side of the table thinking about the coordinates the notemaker had sent. They weren't much help. A google search on the Jitterbug yielded no results, and it became clear that whoever was pulling the strings was having a grand old time. The sender was fucking with us to prove a point. I'd fucked him with the money, and he was fucking us by sending us down random rabbit holes.

To the victor go the spoils.

Devin logged into her meeting and I heard the hubbub of all the reporters. A few piped in at the beginning and after a few minutes a cacophony of voices filled the speakers. There were easily twenty to thirty separate reporters blabbing on about random minutiae. They were getting their cameras ready and talking about their weekends and their kids and the latest binge on TV. It went that way for a good eight minutes before the bigwigs took over.

The bigwigs defined the game. They booked the fights and messed with the purses and the promotion and always put their noses where they didn't belong. But 'twas the game, take it or leave it.

Devin doodled on her notepad while one of the rich promoters announced the card and then yielded the floor to another rich promoter who essentially repeated the same thing as the first promoter. I gripped the table so hard for a second that Devin's computer shook. Fighters were the bedrock of all this shit, and it took so long to get to them. To appreciate them. We risked our lives for good ole entertainment's sake, but the show went on, no questions asked. I wanted to jump in front of the camera and give my best soliloquy of all time, but I let it be.

Devin smiled at me from the other side of the table. Then she made a snoozing gesture.

"They can see that," I said.

Devin shook her head. "My video's off. I'm not turning it on till I'm called. Until then I'll just enjoy my coffee."

She took a sip from her mug.

"Smart girl," I said.

"Easy on the fabric, Hercules. I spill on these keys and it's adios amigos when it comes to that dinero, comprende?"

I understood completely and was impressed with her Spanish.

I went back to my Jitterbug and sent Sims a text. I was picturing ways to fuck up the next press conference I did, and the more I thought about it, the more I wanted to test out Zoom. Of course I enjoyed schooling candy asses in real time, but perhaps things needed to get shaken up for the betterment of the sport. I'd play games in the chats with the media members I didn't like and the sponsors I didn't like, and I'd send the real sharks to breakout rooms that would never end.

I smiled and thought about all the possibilities. Then Henri came over and licked my hand. He waited patiently for a treat, and when he didn't get one he started wrestling with Husker. Their bond was growing, and for a moment I contemplated adopting the chap and bringing him along for all my nomadic adventures. A Doberman on one hip and a husky on the other.

But the thought came and went quick. I was Team Henri all the way. Sorry, Husker. Maybe I'd drop him off at a shelter after all.

The presser finally went to the stars of the hour, and Devin blew it out of the park. She was a natural. At one point in the proceedings she said, "All I want for Christmas is to be number one pound-for-pound badass bitch in the octagon."

The media fired off a gazillion questions. Everything from promotion differences to weight cut to nutrition to mental warfare to the good ole Lone Star State and how it differs from fighting on the coasts. Even though she had it well under control, at times I slipped Devin some zingers and she used them to full effect. At others she simply gave me the finger, tore up my pieces of paper, and went back to her drawings. I counted six so far. Her multi-tasking skills were muy bueno. If Sims was tuning in on the Zoom, he'd be salivating at the prospect of having another trash-talking maestro in his stable. Provided she could back it up in the ring.

The fight game was a bottom-line business after all.

I knew very little about MMA, but I knew the hunger. The eyes never lied. That look of despair and want and destruction. All the greats had it. Devin wanted to shut the assholes up and prove she still had game and prove she still belonged in the club. She was going to do that when the fight went down. I was sure of it.

The media hombres fired off a few more questions, and just like that the presser ended. Devin got up from her chair and stretched.

"We have another one next month right before the real deal," she said. "I couldn't get that one off."

"You'll be ready."

"I hope so."

I got up and took her by the hand. Spontaneity is the name of the game sometimes. We started dancing in the middle of the room. I had no idea what steps we did or whether we were in rhythm. I was a horrible dancer, but I wanted to take Devin's mind off the shit of the day, and for me to use the distraction to think clearly. My brain cells worked like that.

The notemaker hombre was close. A security threat at the

arena. Getting us on Zoom. I could feel it in my bones. The hotel. So much space for destruction.

It added up.

Sure enough, Devin got another text mid-stride, and our dancing ended for the night.

The text read, *Meet you on the rooftop in five.*

23

We went up in three. For one, I wanted to scope out the place, and for another, Devin's suite was already on the top floor so there wasn't far to go. As we stepped out of the room, I took a left and Devin took a right. The dogs tagged along. I walked to the end of the hall and looked for an emergency staircase. Hotels didn't just let any hombre get up to the rooftop. If there was a way up it was through a restricted access avenue.

I found a vending machine, and right next to it was a push door. There was a flashing red exit sign hanging from the ceiling, but nothing about it screamed hotel personnel only. I pushed the door open, and sure enough it led to stairs that went down, not up.

I wondered if any of the other penthouse units had elevators that went to the rooftop. Devin might have negotiated a lower-caliber view with the bigwigs. Sims, by comparison, often stayed in penthouses with elevators that went straight to the lobby as well as straight to the rooftop pool and bar and wherever the hell else his rich ass desired.

I stood there for a few seconds pondering which doorway to hit. There were three on my side, then Devin's unit, then another three on her side. If push came to shove I'd sign some autographs for the unsuspecting guests whose units didn't have the magic elevator.

I walked to the first door and knocked hard.

Nada.

I waited twenty more seconds and did it again.

Nada.

Then I moved to the next door and did the same. No answer. The affluent denizens must have been out at a gala, or perhaps taking in the riverwalk and all its glory. I shook my head and walked to the final door.

Third time's the charm.

But before I could knock, Devin shouted from down the hall.

"Hurry," she said.

I walked as slow as possible to her end of the floor, and when I got there I saw the same exit door and vending machine like on my side. Only difference was the stairs here went up too, and they were gated. A sign read "Authorized Personnel Only," and there was a big ole bolt over the gate that would give even the finest locksmiths a run for their money.

I looked at Devin, and she nodded. She reared back and delivered a crazy kick to the gate. One of the spinniest and quickest kicks I'd ever seen.

Nothing happened.

But if at first you don't succeed, try try again. I tried to imitate Devin's kick, but the best I could do was a floppy round-house. The gate budged maybe a millimeter.

Progress.

Devin kicked again. And again and again.

More progress.

Then she went back to basics.

A teep kick with an ever-so-slight lean-back.

When she delivered it, the bolt snapped and the gate crashed open like a floppy house of cards. She smiled.

We walked up the stairs and pushed open another door. We were on the rooftop. The view was spectacular, but all was quiet.

I took up a fighting stance, and Devin did too. We fanned out in semicircles, me taking the right portion of the rooftop and Devin covering the left, our backs to each other. Teamwork was a beautiful thing. I scanned the right side of the roof inch by inch and saw nothing but soot and rusty metal holding up some water reservoirs. A small ladder led to one of the holding tanks.

I climbed up, undid the valve at the top, and looked inside.

Absolutely nada.

When I came back down I scanned every nook and cranny on my side again and still came up empty.

Another wild goose chase.

I met Devin in the middle of the rooftop and we both shook our heads. We'd been played for sure.

I walked to the edge of the building and looked down. The river was glistening off the sides of the building, and the city lights really looked beautiful at night, even for a small city. I made a pact right then and there to return one day in winter, to see how it all shaped up or if there even was such a thing as a winter in the Lone Star State.

I scanned the side of the building and didn't see anybody hanging from a ledge. I looked across at the few buildings that blocked the sun's rays during the day and I didn't see any Spider-Man hombres there either. I went back to the reservoir side of the building and scanned the side there too. Devin did the same on her side.

We regrouped in the center once again.
It was futile.
But then Devin screamed.
The notemaker was right on time, standing by the steps.
I saw Jake.
Then I saw Sofa again. Or maybe it was his doppelgänger.
And he pressed a gun to Jake's head.

24

"It's a beautiful night for theater, isn't it?" Sofa said. "Acting and staging and delivering are some of the greatest things in all mankind."

He pressed the gun harder against Jake's temple.

I walked a few steps forward. "Put it down, and I'll spare you."

Sofa laughed. "You two are like peas in a pod. Sticking together. Not thinking straight. Fucking everything up."

He looked Devin up and down, the way a player would.

"Back down," I said.

"The champ is here, and he's pissed off." Sofa mocked me and pushed the gun harder into Jake's temple. "It ain't easy being a Saint," he said. "Protecting the masses from the scourge on the streets. Trying to always be one step ahead of the lawman. The drug game ain't what it used to be. All about coin nowadays. Sticking up for what's right. Controlling our little section of the world and adapting, you got it? But one thing that will never adapt is the damned code."

Sofa kicked Jake at the knees, and he buckled to the concrete. Sofa kept the gun on the kid's temple.

Devin stepped closer.

"Honey, don't even think about it."

"The kid has nothing to do with it," I said.

I was looking for an opening, but when the other hombre is armed and you aren't, you need to be the more creative hombre. To avoid looking like Swiss cheese when it's all said and done. I closed my eyes for a second and pictured my plan.

When I opened them I started doing feints with my head and bobbing in and out.

Sofa sneered, and I saw that he had several fillings.

"Kickbacks are kickbacks," Sofa said. "And a contract is a contract. Simple shit. We provided the muscle and they provided the numbers. You feel me, champ? All this jobber had to do over here was take the damned test or hand over the damned answers to the test. And live with the consequences. That's what a jobber does. He puts the needs of the brother-hood above his own."

On some level Sofa was making sense. In pro wrestling terms, the jobber was the dude that came out each night and got squashed to make the other wrestlers look good. The money guys. The superstars. He took a dive to build up the cred of others. It was no different than the jobbers that often filled the boxing world. So many hombres were undefeated after twenty fights because they'd fought shitty opponents to build up their brand. Not moi. I wanted to fight anybody and everybody. I didn't give a shit about records.

But Jake had special needs. Jobber or no jobber, it wasn't the same. Sofa was too consumed.

"And everybody profits and gets to feed their families like civilized people at the end of the day," Sofa continued. "Simple operation. The Saints are all about simple. Money."

Devin moved closer to Sofa.

"Honey, I said don't try me," he said. "I know you like to run around them cages and all, but I've had enough excitement for today. You know how tough it is to find the right chemicals to mimic blood and to hold in my breathing while the two of youse traipse around my fucking place? And then take my dog too."

"Husker deserves so much more," Devin said.

"Fuck you, bitch."

Jake tried to say something, but Sofa pistol-whipped him and he fell face down on the concrete. Sofa kept the gun trained on him.

Devin shouted, but Sofa was in his own world. That's how criminal hombres rolled. I was so used to that milieu, it was like riding a bike.

It was in that moment that I knew I was going to tackle his ass. It was the only play. I'd wait for a sliver of an opening and then I'd charge. I couldn't box my way out of this one. Or even kick my way out of it. I had to tackle his ass and hope the gun didn't discharge right in my face in the process.

Sims wouldn't be happy with that.

Sofa walked a few steps back from Jake, taking the gun off him for just a moment. He looked out at the water, smiled, then trained the gun back on the kid.

I waited.

"When the jobber sings on top of it, that's the final straw. Singing is believing, as they say. Can't have that ruin our business model, can we? This boy wanna bring down this whole shit. I don't fuckin' think so. Where's the money, Gedrin?"

I had left the bag down by the gate that Devin had tuned up.

"And don't give me fake-ass bills like last time. You celebs make so much and are so fucking cheap. You want free samples and free gift baskets all day. You think you run this town. You fly first class in and out whenever you please and collect a check, huh?"

"I fly coach, hombre."

Truth be told I flew more than first class. I took Sims's private jet whenever the hell I pleased. But who was keeping score? Plus, I needed my opening.

"The bag's by the stairs," I said.

"Your doggie trained to fetch or is he trying to hump my doggie?"

"Fuck you," I said. "Henri is a good citizen. He doesn't concern himself with matters of the flesh."

"Rex, bag," he shouted.

I had no idea what Sofa was saying. But then he repeated it, and Husker sprinted up the stairs to the roof with the duffel bag in his mouth.

"Rex, open."

Husker pulled the zipper on the bag, and the bills started falling out.

Sofa smiled so wide I could see five fillings.

"The most loyal creatures in the world, these ones. You can teach them anything you want them to. How to fetch. How to shit on cue. How to give a paw. And how to play possum. Rex is good at that."

He looked at Rex, and Rex heeled at his side like an obedient dog would with its owner.

Henri came up the stairs a few seconds later and heeled at my side. He knew something was up because he didn't try to play with Rex. He stared at him across the way and didn't back down. I had trained Henri well. Not opening duffel zippers well, but well in all the ways that counted.

I rubbed his whiskers.

"Let the kid go and I'll give all the Saints my John Hancock. Free of charge," I said.

Sofa scoffed. "That shit ain't worth the paper it's printed on. You shoulda signed with Anton way back when you had the chance. All our pockets would be deeper, man. Instead you had to butcher some girl on the side of the road and beat the case. Lucky you never saw a Saint on the inside."

Truth be told I *had* encountered a Saint at Pontiac. But he was too much of a pussy to talk shit to my face or throw down. I was ready for him, but it takes two to tango.

"Rex, get him."

Rex morphed from the happy-go-lucky chap I'd known the last couple hours to a beast incarnate. He sprinted toward Henri with his jaws out and his nostrils flared.

But Henri was ready for it. A dog's intuition rivals a woman's any day of the week.

As Rex tried to bite Henri, Henri swatted him away like a fly. They chased each other around the roof, Rex trying to get Henri in the ass and Henri trying to get Rex wherever the hell he pleased.

I smiled.

I had found my opening.

I did a swan dive at Sofa and tackled him to the ground. The gun flew out of his hands, and Jake ran for cover.

Sofa got up and we traded blows. He was good, and I was running out of mileage. He got me with a nice left hook and a body shot that sent me to the ground. Then he picked up the duffel bag and ran down the stairs.

As I clutched my liver, I saw Devin running after him.

25

I hobbled to the steps, but gravity was not my best friend. A liver shot was one of the worst shots in the fight game. I'd rather be knocked out than feel my insides curl up and flex all wrong.

I fell down the steps, and my back felt like a million shards of glass had pierced it.

I got to my feet and shouted Henri's name. I thought he was still on the rooftop, but all was quiet.

Nada.

I did it again, and then some residents started coming out of their penthouses. I wanted to bitch at them for not opening up earlier, but I let it be. I waved them off, clutched my side, and fell down again.

I got up, and this time Jake was at my side. He held me up.

"Gedrin, you're the man. Come on."

The kid hoisted me under one arm, and we made our way down the hall to the elevator. He had fresh cuts above both his eyebrows and his elbows looked like shit too, but the kid was tough as nails. I didn't ask any questions and he didn't give any answers. The only thing left was to find Devin.

Jake wiped his blood with his shirt. "That asshole better not touch my sister," he said.

I nodded. "When I'm done with him he won't be using his hands ever again. Now can you dig that?"

Jake knew the pro wrestling reference, smiled, and filled in the rest.

"Sucka!"

The elevator hit our floor and we took it down to the lobby. The concierge started to bid us a good evening, but when he saw what shape we were in he looked flabbergasted.

We ignored him and walked outside. Sofa had probably gotten on his Harley and gotten the hell out of Dodge. Anybody with twenty mill in liquid assets and half a brain would do the same. But then again, Sofa was a shot caller who didn't want to draw attention to himself. Maybe he'd hopped on the riverwalk in order to flag a cab further down.

We tried the riverwalk.

At first we passed nothing but tourists clutching their sangrias, jovially taking in the San Antonio night scene. But then twenty paces ahead we hit pay dirt. Devin was walking slowly, methodically. Every few paces she'd stare out over the water. I couldn't see Sofa anywhere in the distance, but if she put something in her mind she'd get it no questions asked. No way she would let the trail go cold.

Game over.

I pointed her out to Jake and we stayed the course, tailing from behind at half speed. Sofa had given me a damned good body shot and I was impressed that I was still feeling the effects. Sal had told me to never underestimate my opponent, yet I always did.

Pride cometh before the fall.

We caught up to Devin one hundred and twenty seconds later. But the tables had turned. She wasn't walking or running or in pursuit of anyone anymore. She was in an alley a few paces off the main touristy fare, and Sofa had a knife to her throat.

"You couldn't let sleeping dogs lie, could you?" Sofa said. "Hasn't your mama ever told you not to mess with those who are far more qualified than you in the pain-giving business?"

I gritted my teeth and clenched my fists.

Sofa smiled.

"Where'd you train at?" I said.

"I don't do that boxing shit. That's for little bitches. Muay Thai and BJJ black belt. That's my thing. Given to me from the original Gracie. You never know when you might need to defend yourself on these streets."

My head was still spinning, but that explained it. Sofa had the tools to keep me at a distance, twist me up in a pretzel whenever he wanted, and land strategic shots.

Sal would be proud.

I'd met my match.

"The pain business is for the young 'uns," I said.

I put my hands up in a surrender position. Sofa didn't buy it. I was hoping that would have triggered Devin to make her move, but she stayed quiet, like she'd been held up at knifepoint a million times before and it was just another walk in the park for her.

I knew she was well trained in the art of jiujitsu and could definitely strike, but perhaps trying to get out of the chokehold of a black belt would only lead to a stronger chokehold. Especially when you're up against the knife.

"The jobbers are what's wrong with this world," Sofa said. "Can't ever get them to do the job right. So that means we gotta up the ante now, don't we? To teach them a lesson. What's better than a bag full of change? How 'bout two? You have one hour, Gedrin, to get me another bag. Ten mill is an acceptable sum for the shit you and that fucking kid have put me through. When the feds want your ass they will never stop. The lam sounds great right now. Teach that jobber some manners, and I'm keeping this little slut all to myself until you—"

Jake fired right into Sofa's head and his brain exploded all over the pavement.

Devin sprinted to Jake, and they hugged for so long I'm not gonna lie: I had some waterworks. Neither let go. Family is family.

I did what I did best in these situations. I cleaned up. I took the gun from where Jake dropped it. It was Sofa's gun; Jake must have swiped it before coming down the stairs after me. I wiped it down, then went back to Sofa's body and made it look the way it was supposed to look.

For family.

Then I called Sims and heard sirens in the distance.

26

"If you miss the ferry, I'm telling them you were the aggressor," Sims said. "Don't fucking try me."

Devin, Jake, and I were walking back to the hotel, licking our wounds. In typical lawyer-agent fashion, Sims had cleared everything up with the authorities. I gave a brief statement on scene to some non-khaki boys and got the hella outta Dodge. It helps when the two victims on a case are celebrities, and eyewitnesses have cell phone video of an alley shitshow. We signed some autographs, posed for some pictures, and let the coroner handle the rest.

"Let's watch *Smackdown*," Jake said.

I looked at my Jitterbug and saw the time.

"Main event finished an hour ago."

"I like the clips online," Jake said. "I can watch all the entrances again and again and then the finishers."

"All right, buddy, let's do it."

Jake smiled and gave me a hug. I didn't have an objection.

Devin squeezed my hand.

"You're good with him," she said. "You'd make a great big brother, little brother."

"Talk to my agent."

She laughed and punched me in the shoulder. We walked hand in hand the whole way back. Jake made *ew* sounds at first, but eventually he accepted it and let us be. Henri joined us midway through too. The rascal always knew how to put on a show. I'd shouted his name on scene several times, and I guess my voice had penetrated through the ether and found its destination. He looked fine, with nary a scratch. I had no idea where Rex was, and I didn't care. I had my boy and that was all that mattered.

When we got back to the hotel, I watched some Rock promos with Jake. He took out his tablet and casted the clips onto the big screen, and we had a great time. The kid really looked down on the new-era stuff, which made me respect him even more. We watched so many classics that I felt like my brain cells were regenerating.

Eventually Jake fell asleep and Devin and I went to the other bedroom and got in some cardio. We'd been through one hell of a day, and we went at it like our lives depended on it. Slowly. Tenderly. Sweet. Sensual. Devin wanted more and more and so did I. We had so many rounds that by the end my head was spinning again.

We collapsed in each other's arms and lay there for a while. Lost in thought, pondering things that were best suited for pondering. 'Twas the ways things usually happened in the love department. Both parties inevitably came to a point where the topic of the future cropped up. Stay the course or abort. It was as simple as that, though the reasons were anything but.

I didn't have to say anything to Devin because she said it to me first. Things wouldn't be the same as before. She had a fight coming up and I had my camp coming up. She was on one coast and I enjoyed all coasts.

Story of my life.

Maybe one day we'd meet up again and have some fun and reminisce as only two celebrities can. But until then it was a mutual, respectful parting of the ways.

Devin teared up a little, but that's what she wanted in the end.

"Sims is signing you, win or lose," I said.

"He better."

She kissed me, and we had one final round. We saved the best for last.

27

The next day Henri and I were at the Sand Dunes in Colorado. I'd booked a very expensive cab to get there and put it on Sims's tab. Apparently his jet was undergoing routine maintenance and was temporarily out of commission.

The ride had been worth it. The dunes, which stretched for roughly thirty miles, were the highest sand mountains in all of North America. Rumor had it the tallest dune was close to seven hundred fifty feet. As I gazed out at the landscape, I smiled. We were all little crustaceans against the backdrop of nature's beauty. The wonders of the world never ceased to amaze me.

Now I stood among the dunes with Henri, stretching my neck and closing my eyes as the sun baked my forehead. I had no idea what this next camp would bring, but I knew it would be one hell of a ride. Lose the next fight and I could kiss my title goodbye. Win it and I'd be immortalized among the greats. The comeback story complete.

I took a tennis ball out of my pocket and tossed it down the dunes. Henri sprinted after it like it was the best steak of all time. He fetched it in a heartbeat. We did that for a while, then I gave the fur monster some water and plenty of pets.

My phone rang. I was expecting Sims to chide me some more about my antics in the Lone Star State, but this time it was Sal.

"Boyo, no sex till after the fight."

"Yessir."

"I mean it, dammit. Weak legs, easy target. Simba tells me everything. And you best get your ass on the ferry tomorrow. I got plenty of snacks for the ride. Devil's door will straighten you up, don't worry. This Mado guy is a machine. He's got a right hook from hell and a slick jab."

I hadn't done any homework on Mado, but then again I never did any homework on my opponents, and Sal always chided me for it. The way I saw it, I'd just beat the hell out of whoever was in front of me and get the belt I never lost.

Easy peasy.

"You got pancakes on that ferry?" I said.

"Boyo, you win the title, I'll buy you a whole damned pancake factory."

Muy bueno.

I gave Henri one of his favorite treats and I stayed outta trouble.

AUTHOR'S NOTE

Thanks for reading! I hope you enjoyed the Gedrin universe just as much as I enjoyed writing it. I would greatly appreciate it if you would leave a review on Amazon. Reviews allow more readers to find Gedrin, and this ultimately allows me to keep writing stories that I hope will leave an indelible footprint in our literary world.

—Greg

ACKNOWLEDGMENTS

Thank you to my team. Writing may be a solitary endeavor, but publishing is certainly a collective one. Thank you to my beta reader Bailee Myers. Your early insights really helped whip Gedrin into shape.

Thank you to my editor David Gatewood for making my prose shine. Thank you to my proofreader Donna Rich for snagging those pesky typos. Thank you to my cover designers at Deranged Doctor Design. I'm blown away by all the Gedrin covers and this one is no different.

And of course thank you to all those who have shaped my writing indirectly in some way. It's impossible to mention everybody here, but y'all know who you are.

ALSO BY GREG GOUNTANIS

THE LANCE GEDRIN SERIES

The Night Contract (Lance Gedrin #1)

The Fink (Lance Gedrin #2)

The Loran (Lance Gedrin #3)

The Jobber (Lance Gedrin #4)

The Lance Gedrin Box Set (Books 1-4)

JOIN GREG'S NEWSLETTER

For the latest updates on Greg's writing, sign up for his newsletter at: https://dashboard.mailerlite.com/forms/1415379/150624884207126495/share

ABOUT THE AUTHOR

Greg Gountanis writes mysteries and thrillers filled with a lot of action, wit, and courtroom drama. When he's not writing, he's lawyering. For over a decade, Greg's worked as a public defender in Chicago.

Get the latest news on Greg's books at www.greggountanis.com and on social media.

facebook.com/GregGountanisAuthor

amazon.com/stores/author/B08P1C58RR

youtube.com/greggountanis

www.ingramcontent.com/pod-product-compliance
Lightning Source LLC
Chambersburg PA
CBHW051923240626
47153CB00004B/1347